PRAISE FOR **The Warhol Gang**

"Pitched somewhere between the terse, absurdist nihilism of Chuck (*Fight Club*) Palahniuk and the anesthetized apocalypticism of J.G. (*Crash*) Ballard." —*Toronto Star*

"A brilliant, brutal evocation of contemporary life, less a satire than it is a warning. Darbyshire writes with an unflinching clarity, in a minimalist, nay, brutalist style that doesn't allow the reader to look away. . . . Exhilarating." —*Edmonton Journal*

"*The Warhol Gang* is a nightmare that will linger for days."
—*Telegraph-Journal* (Saint John)

"A stunning new novel." —*The Star Phoenix*

"An action-packed, rollicking story that serves as a biting satire of consumerism, capitalism, affluenza, and fame. . . . Echoes not only of Palahniuk but of Oliver Stone's *Natural Born Killers* and David Cronenberg's adaptation of J.G. Ballard's novel *Crash*."
—*Quill & Quire*

"A disorienting (and chest-thumping) take on consumer culture. . . . A riveting story told in Palahniuk-spare sentences that rattle like machine-gun fire around your head, and it is also highly recommended." —*Eye Weekly*

"Wow! No one has written a book this brainy, heartfelt, and absurd in a while. The whole idea is insane, and the comic plot is laced with brilliant wit and wisdom."
—Lee Henderson, author of *The Man Game*

The Warhol Gang

THE WARHOL GANG

PETER DARBYSHIRE

HARPER
PERENNIAL

The Warhol Gang
Copyright © 2010 by Peter Darbyshire.
All rights reserved.

Published by Harper Perennial, an imprint of HarperCollins Publishers Ltd

First published in Canada in a hardcover edition by HarperCollins Publishers Ltd: 2010
This Harper Perennial trade paperback edition: 2011

HarperCollins books may be purchased for educational, business,
or sales promotional use through our Special Markets Department.

HarperCollins Publishers Ltd
2 Bloor Street East, 20th Floor
Toronto, Ontario, Canada
M4W 1A8

www.harpercollins.ca

Library and Archives Canada Cataloguing in Publication
information is available upon request

ISBN: 978-1-55468-077-1

Printed and bound in the United States

RRD 10 9 8 7 6 5 4 3 2 1

Everything ends in the Ikea.

The cops crouch behind barricades they've assembled in the showroom. Wardrobes dragged over from fake bedroom suites. Oversized shopping bags full of pillows and sofa cushions. Trolleys stacked with boxes brought in from the warehouse area. They aim their assault rifles and handguns and loudspeakers at the door to the Ikea staff room. Someone has spray-painted the word Resist! on the door.

I watch the scene from behind the cops. Customers lie on the floor at my feet, using display bins of candles and empty photo frames for cover. They hold phones over their heads to film the action, like a concert. I hold the gun Flint gave me in my hand.

A woman's voice over the PA says the store is closing and everyone should proceed to the cash registers. That's when the door to the staff room opens. I wait for Holiday to step out but instead it's Paris. She looks just like she does on her show. There's no sign of Holiday at all. Paris holds her hands behind her back, like she's handcuffed. But she's not.

"No," I say, because I know what's about to happen. I want her to turn around and go back inside the staff room. But instead she just smiles as she looks at all the people watching her. The cops relax and smile back. A couple of them even wave.

"The Warhol Gang has let Paris go," the reporter says from behind her barricade. A crib stuffed to the top with plastic babies.

A cop with a bandage around his head steps out from behind a full-length mirror and reaches for Paris. It's Flint. But Flint is dead. I should know. I killed him.

Paris raises her right hand from behind her back. She's holding the same gun I'm holding. "You are not alone," she says and shoots Flint in the head. He falls back into the mirror, taking it to the ground with him. It shatters and some of the pieces land at my feet. I look for my reflection. I can't see anything but the products on the shelves around me. Bedsheets in packages. Curtain rods. Clothes hangers.

Everyone starts screaming, and the reporter turns to her camera and says, "Paris has joined the Warhol Gang!" Then the cops open fire and Paris spins around and hits the wall. A loudspeaker shrieks. Paris slumps to the floor, leaving a smear of blood on the wall. Like an abstract print in the Ikea's art section.

For a moment, no one moves. It's as if someone's hit pause. Then I try to shoot the cops, but nothing happens when I pull the trigger. I'm out of ammo. No one even looks at me. All I can do is watch a man wearing a Warhol mask and Ikea uniform come out of the staff room and return fire with the gun Paris dropped. I don't know who he is. Everyone dives for cover and the man drags Paris away, slamming the door shut. The cops pop back up and start shooting again, through the wall, through Paris's blood. The bullet holes form words.

Payless Tactical—make each shot count!

Then the hologram fades and I'm left standing alone in an empty room. Nothing but blank walls and a hallway that leads to the next You're History Experience.

No Ikea.

No Paris.

No Flint.

No Holiday.

I'm not even sure I'm there.

Rewind three months.

I work for Adsenses, a market-research company. I have a code name at work. Trotsky. The office supervisor, a man named Nickel, gives it to me my first day. When I step out of the elevator, he's waiting for me with an adhesive name tag he puts on my chest. He smiles as he does it. Nickel is one of those managers who never stops smiling.

"That's not my name," I point out.

"It's your name now," Nickel says, smoothing the edges of the name tag to make sure it sticks. "All the temps get code names."

"I'm a temp?" I ask.

"Aren't you?" Nickel asks.

I think back to what the woman at the placement agency had said. She'd asked all the standard questions about where I saw myself in a year, if I ever viewed porn at work, if I ever thought about doing harm to my co-workers or myself, and I'd answered with all the standard lies. But I couldn't recall anything about being a temp.

"I don't know," I say.

"I don't know either," Nickel says. He stares at the wall around the elevator while he thinks about it. The wall is a video ad. It shows a beach somewhere. When you step into the elevator, it's like you're walking into the ocean. The clouds are words, the name of a travel agency. Club Escape. A naked woman walks into the water from the edge of the screen. At least, I think she's naked. Parts of her are pixelated. She swims away from me, out to the horizon. I wonder if she's CGI or real. I hope she's real.

"What's everyone else who works here?" I ask. "Are they temps?"

"I'll request a memo for clarification," Nickel says, like he hasn't heard my question.

I finger the name tag. The ink from the marker is still wet and smudges under my touch.

"Who's Trotsky anyway?" I ask.

"It's random," Nickel says. "All the code names are random." He peels the name tag from my chest and makes me a new one with unsmudged letters.

"Why can't we just be ourselves?" I ask as Nickel puts the new name tag on my chest, in the exact same spot as the last one. He's so accurate I wonder how many people he's given name tags.

"I'm not sure what you mean," Nickel says.

"Why do we need code names?" I ask.

"We have to remove as much of your life from the process as possible," Nickel says. "Your name, your clothes. Everything that tells you who you are. We don't want anything to come between you and the products." He pauses, then adds, "We're still working on the memories."

The woman in the water disappears behind a wave. I can't see her anywhere now.

"So what's your code name?" I ask.

"Nickel," Nickel says.

"What's your real name?" I ask.

"Nickel," Nickel says.

Adsenses is on the eighteenth floor of an office tower downtown. The building has many more floors—it goes to sixty or seventy, maybe higher. I don't really know. The elevators end at the fiftieth floor, but a sign on a wall of the lobby says there are more elevators up there that go to the private floors. Other elevators go down into the mall beneath the city.

Posters around the office show oceans and forests and deserts and tell everyone to Imagine, but they don't say what to Imagine. I've never been to any place like those shown in the posters. I've never been outside of the city.

When I look out over the cubicles I can see the building across the street. It's identical to the one I work in. The windows of both towers are mirrored glass, and they reflect each other reflecting each other. I get dizzy if I look at the other building too long. Sometimes when I walk through the office I wonder if there's someone like me over there.

When I look past the office tower across the street, I can see my apartment building a half dozen blocks away, on the other side of some parking garages. It's connected to the mall as well. I can take the underground tunnels from home to work and back again without ever leaving the mall. I live so close, if I bought a rifle I could shoot people in my office without even getting out of bed, like that amputee sniper who was killing joggers a few months back.

I work in Adsenses' neuromarketing department. Each day, Nickel leads me to a room with a scanner called the pod. It's like one of those full-body MRI machines you see in medical shows, only it has a door that locks you inside. Nickel says it was developed by the military for interrogations. Nickel tells me to strip off all my clothes. I put them in a recycling bin he then takes away. I'm not sure what he does with them. I'm not sure I want to know.

I lie on a sliding bed that Nickel pushes into the pod. When he closes and seals the door, I try not to scream. I learn on my first day that screaming doesn't do any good. Nickel doesn't let me out. Nickel says he knows it's frightening, but the pod is where we learn to face ourselves. Nickel says the pod is where we learn who we really are.

The ads are projected from somewhere into the pod, a few inches over my face. Holograms. Nickel says the products in them don't exist yet. Nickel says they're only someone else's fantasies at this point. Nickel says whether or not they become real depends on me.

"When you're in the pod, you're the most powerful person in the world," Nickel tells me at one point while I lie in the darkness. I can't tell where the speaker is. It sounds like his voice is in my head. "You make the world," Nickel adds.

"Aren't there other people who do this?" I ask.

"You're each the most powerful person in your own world," Nickel says.

It's true: I'm powerful when I imagine myself using the products. Only it's not me.

A home espresso maker floats in the darkness above me.

I imagine a cup of espresso sitting on a marble counter. A kitchen with gleaming appliances, including the espresso maker. A woman sitting at the kitchen island, sipping the espresso.

A phone floats in the darkness above me.

I imagine the woman putting down the espresso and answering her phone. The same phone that floats above me. I imagine the rest of the condo as she talks about a trip to the spa with someone. The furniture is a shade of white I didn't realize was possible. Jazz plays through hidden speakers somewhere. Floor-to-ceiling windows overlook the city. The sort of place that costs a fortune.

A mirror floats in the darkness above me.

I imagine the mirror hanging on the wall above the couch. I look at myself in it. I'm wearing a suit, a tie. A gold wedding band. I talk on my phone. The same one that the woman talks on. I have a haircut that looks like it cost hundreds of dollars. Only it's not me. I'm someone else, a man I've never seen before. Darker hair than mine, taller, more muscular. I try to imagine myself—the real me—in his place, but I can't.

He doesn't last anyway. Another product makes him fade away.

A laser pointer floats in the darkness above me.

I try to imagine myself using it, but now I'm a different man in a different suit and tie. Tanned skin and manicured nails. I stand at the end of a table in a conference room and use the pointer to highlight graphs in a presentation projected onto the wall. Everyone seated around the table watches me and waits for me to tell them what's important. I forget the other man. I forget myself.

The walls of the pod are too close for me to raise my arms. I can't touch the holograms. All I can do is watch them fade in and out of existence.

When Nickel lets me out of the pod and I remember who I am again, I feel an actual hollowness inside, like something in me has gone missing.

I remember I live in a one-bedroom apartment, not a penthouse.

I remember I'm single, not married.

I remember I'm lying naked in a pod, not at a job that requires a suit and tie.

Once, I ask Nickel what the researchers are looking for. He gives me back my clothes—jeans, casual shirt, no jewellery—and watches me get dressed, then leads me into the control room. The walls are lined with monitors. Each one shows an image of a different brain, with glowing numbers floating in the brains.

"We study everything," Nickel tells me. "We watch your heart rate, your breathing, how much you sweat. If you get an erection, we measure it." He takes me over to one of the brains. It's mostly dark, with little spots of light that flare up here and there and then fade away. The pattern of the lights looks random.

"Is that me?" I ask.

"This is you," Nickel says, tapping the dark parts of the brain. He points to a yellow spot that glows briefly on one side of the brain. "This is you thinking about the product."

"That's good, right?" I ask.

"It's good, but it's not optimal," Nickel says.

"What would be optimal?" I ask.

Nickel watches another flare. "Optimal would be if that was your entire brain," he says. He turns off the monitor and I disappear.

I spend my breaks with the men from the pods in the rooms around me. Nickel says we're a team, although I'm not sure what actually makes us a team. Maybe they see the same products I do in their pods. I wonder if they imagine the same things I do.

There are three of them besides me: Nader, who ran a tech-support call centre until the jobs were outsourced to a prison; Thatcher, a former auto mechanic with a melted face who has to speak through a voice box because a car caught fire while he was working on it; and Reagan, a former insurance agent who was laid off and who keeps saying this job is only temporary for him. He says he wants another job but the placement agency won't give him one, and Thatcher and Nader nod in agreement. I hope they don't have the same placement agency as me, but I'm afraid to ask.

We pass the time by wandering other floors in the building, through offices that have been abandoned, their doors left propped open, their locks turned off. We sit in empty cubicles and look at stray memos or invoices we find in drawers. We try to guess from them what the companies did.

An order form for erasable markers.

A debt-counselling firm, Nader says.

A memo reminding people about the office dress code.

An investment company, Thatcher says.

A sheet of paper with a list of names on it, all crossed out.

A market-research company, Reagan says.

We sit in a staff room that's identical to the staff room in our office, only the vending machines in this one are empty and the monitors on the wall don't work. I ask the others what they see in their pods.

Reagan says he dreams he's won the lottery and can actually afford to buy all the products we see.

"You wouldn't believe the mansion I live in," he says. "It's got everything they've ever shown me."

Thatcher says he sees the past, back before the accident with the car took his life away from him. He says he's still with his wife, living in his old house. He says it's furnished with the products from the pod instead of what he actually owned. He says he can't recognize himself anymore.

"I know it's supposed to be me," he says, "but when I see him . . ." His voice trails off into static.

Nader says he can never imagine himself at all, no matter how hard he tries.

"Like you're someone else?" I ask, but he shakes his head.

"It's like I'm floating outside the scene," he says. "Like I'm not real."

"Like an out-of-body experience," I say. I've seen shows online about that kind of thing. People say they see God or Jesus, but the doctors say it's just the brain misfiring. Like when you remember something as it's happening, or when you fall in love.

"I think it's more like I'm a ghost," he says.

He asks me what I see but I shake my head. "I think there's something wrong with my pod," I say. I don't want to tell them what I really see. I don't want them to think there's something wrong with me. I'm not even sure yet if there's something wrong with me.

When we're done talking about the products, we don't have much left to say to each other. I ask them their real names, but they won't tell me.

"We're not allowed to reveal them," Thatcher says. "It's in the contract."

"What do you mean?" I ask. I signed the contract without reading it.

"We have to stay in character," Reagan says.

"Or we get fined," Nader adds.

"Character?" I ask.

"You know, who you're supposed to be now," Thatcher says.

I don't know who I'm supposed to be now, so I change the subject. I ask them how they wound up at Adsenses.

"We all made the same mistake as you," Reagan says.

"What mistake?" I ask.

"If we knew that, we wouldn't be here," Reagan says. He punches buttons on one of the empty vending machines but nothing happens.

We can't think of anything else to say, so we just go back to Adsenses and let Nickel lock us in our pods again.

Sometimes I practise conversations at night so my co-workers will talk to me more. I use people in the news videos online as stand-ins for them. I wish I had some friends I could talk to, like in the comedy shows, but there's no one. The only friends I ever have are co-workers at my jobs, and I'm too new at Adsenses to be friends with anyone yet.

A sports commentator complains about a baseball team losing a game.

"Just keep watching," I say.

A woman cries for her missing daughter at a press conference.

"Don't worry, she's out there somewhere," I say.

A cop lies on a hospital bed, bandages around his chest, and tells a reporter about how he'd been shot. He'd seen a white light in the darkness, but then it had drifted away from him and he'd woken up screaming in the hospital bed.

"I know what you mean," I say.

I feel worse with each shift at Adsenses.

A laptop floats in the darkness above me.

I imagine I'm an older man sitting in a café somewhere with palm trees, checking my bank account online. There's more money in it than I've ever had in my real life. There's more money in it than I'll ever have.

A patio chair floats in the darkness above me.

I imagine I'm a man around my age sitting on the chair beside a pool. I imagine myself with a tan, with washboard abs. I imagine watching a woman swim beneath the surface of the water.

An empty photo frame floats in the darkness above me.

I can't imagine anything at all. My mind goes blank. Like a frozen computer. I wonder if something inside me has crashed.

When Nickel lets me out of the pod, I'm unable to stand for a moment. I'm dizzy. I look down at my pale body, my soft stomach. I feel a wave of nausea at the sight of myself. I want to be the men I imagined myself to be in the pod, but I don't know how.

"I'm not sure this is the right job for me," I tell Nickel.

"I've seen inside a lot of minds in my time here," Nickel says, "and if there's anyone who's a natural, it's you."

I wander the mall to distract myself from whatever's wrong with me. The mall's tunnels go everywhere in the city—under the streets, up through walkways connecting office towers, into bus-station lobbies and hospital cafeterias. I don't think the mall has a beginning or an end. The mall is a part of everything or maybe everything is a part of the mall. Whatever I need is in the mall. Food courts. Clothing stores. Cinemas. I never have to leave the mall.

People at past jobs have told me there are secret levels to the mall. Underground gardens tended by communes of homeless people. Penthouse bars where supermodels have sex parties. Abandoned tunnels where squatters occupy empty stores and sell stolen goods for a fraction of their normal price. Nobody I've met has ever seen any of these things in person, but they've all heard of someone who's been there.

I go to one of the mall's artificial beaches. It's in between an Army Recruiting Store and a PharmaWorld. I go into the PharmaWorld and ask one of the roaming pharmacists for help.

"I'm having trouble seeing myself properly," I say.

"Mirrors are in the Home Dreams section," he says.

"No, I mean in my head," I tell him. "When I imagine myself, it's not really me."

"That could be caused by anything," the pharmacist says but sells me a bottle of white pills. He tells me the dosage is one a day. "If you take more than that, we're not responsible for what happens," he says.

I go into the change room at the beach and take two of the pills. I've taken so many different pills, my body's developed immunities to half of them.

I put on my swimsuit and lock up my clothes, then wade out in the water. It's as warm as a bath. I float there for a while, staring up at the video screens of the blue sky overhead. I feel empty inside after taking the pills, but it's a different kind of emptiness than when I leave the pod. I just feel nothing at all. I think I could float there forever, not thinking about anything, but then the artificial shark comes out of its underwater cave and starts attacking people.

I've been at this beach before and know the shark is supposed to swim near people but veer away when it gets too close. It has sensors and algorithms and all that. It's only supposed to scare you. But this time it heads straight for an older couple in inflatable chairs and rams them. Their chairs burst and they sink into the water. The shark moves on to the next closest person, a woman wearing water wings. She thrashes and screams but it swims right over her, pushing her under. That's when I realize something is wrong with the shark's programming. Or maybe it's been hacked. I see someone has spray-painted the word Resist! on the side of the shark.

People in the water scream and head for the shore, and then the shark bumps me as it goes past, spinning me around. Its eyes swivel back to watch me, unblinking, as it swims on. I wonder what it sees when it looks at me.

I wish I'd bought pills to make me afraid, so I could be like everyone else. I think about going back to the PharmaWorld, but I figure by the time I returned to the water, the shark would probably be in its cave again.

I go back to the change room instead and find all the lockers broken open. My clothes are still there, but my wallet is gone. My pills are still in my pocket though, so I take another one. I reach for my phone to cancel my credit cards, but my phone is gone, too. I'm trying to decide what to do next when a pair of men in matching swimsuits walk into the change room and start swearing at the sight of the open lockers. I leave before they think I'm responsible. I'm in such a hurry to get out of there I forget my swimsuit on the bench.

Back in the mall, I wander from store to store. I know I should be getting new credit cards and a new phone and new swimsuit, but I'm feeling too relaxed from the pills to worry about it right now. I find myself in some sort of antique shop with several rooms. I look at old suits of armour inside glass cases. I look at dinosaur bones on pedestals. I look at painted wooden masks hanging on a wall. I read the product information on the signs beside the masks. It says they're totems that transform their wearers into powerful beings. I can't see price tags on any of them, so I take one of the masks from the wall and turn it over. There's no price on that side either. I put the mask on to see what I become, but I don't feel any different.

I don't hear the alarm until the security guards walk into the room. I wonder how long it's been ringing. The security guards wear name tags, but their name tags are blank. One of them shakes his head at me. The other one takes the mask from me and puts it back on the wall. The alarms stop.

"I wasn't trying to steal it," I explain. "I was just looking for a price. I don't know why that alarm went off."

"The alarm went off because you're in a museum, not a shop," the guard who replaced the mask says. The other one just shakes his head some more.

"I think I'm lost," I admit. I look around for an exit, but the guards grab me and drag me through a door marked Staff.

"I want to go back to the mall," I tell them.

"You haven't left it," the one who spoke says.

I try to break free, but the guards don't seem to notice. They probably take the pills that make you strong. I give up. I let them lead me where they want.

They take me down a hall littered with dead cockroaches to a room that's empty except for a door in each of the walls. The walls are white but the doors are black. One of the doors leads to an interrogation room. A table, two metal chairs, a security camera mounted on the ceiling. Its lens is just like the shark's eyes.

"I just wanted to go to the beach," I say.

"Is this your official statement?" the guard who spoke before asks. The other guard pushes me into one of the chairs, then asks my name.

"Trotsky," I tell him.

He shakes his head at me again and goes through my pockets,

THE WARHOL GANG 21

looking for my wallet. But all he finds are the pills. He opens the bottle and looks at them.

"It was them," I say, nodding at the pills. "I didn't know where I was."

"You should take those pills that help you concentrate," the other guard says. "They might remind you where you are."

"I tried those once," I say. "They gave me nightmares."

He nods like he understands.

The guard searching me puts the pills back in my pocket.

"So you don't have a name," he says. "No wallet. No ID. No credit cards."

"That's right," I say.

"A nobody," he says. "You don't even exist."

I don't say anything. I don't like the way this is going. I've seen the cop shows online.

But they don't say anything either. They just stare at me. I look up at the security camera. I can't tell if it's recording or not. I hope it is. I think they won't do anything too bad to me if it's recording.

Finally, I ask if I'm free to go.

They nod simultaneously. "But we'd better not see you again," the one who searched me says. "If we do, we'll disappear you."

"Disappear me?" I ask.

"Like an abortion," the other one says.

I get up and leave the room, but I can't remember the way back to the mall. I try a door at random. I'm in a hallway lined with dead cockroaches. I think I'm going the right way until

I reach the end of the hallway and enter a large room filled with industrial-sized dumpsters. The dumpsters are overflowing with products. Monitors with broken screens. Bicycles with bent frames. Office chairs with collapsed seats. I suddenly feel sick, like I'm going to throw up. My heart starts to pound. I worry I'm having a heart attack. I see a dumpster full of headless mannequins and run back the way I came, into the interrogation room. It's empty now, but I think the camera swivels my way.

I keep running. This time I find a hallway that leads back to the mall, with all its lights and people and stores with windows full of healthy mannequins. I forget about the security guards and the interrogation. My heart beats at a normal speed again. I go back to thinking about nothing at all.

I see hundreds of products in the pod every day. I imagine myself as hundreds of better men in the pod every day. When I get out for breaks and remember who I really am, I feel dizzier and more nauseous every day.

And I start to see things from the pod outside the pod.

A suit floats in the darkness above me.

Nickel pulls me from the pod. I don't know where I am for a moment. I can't remember my name. I'm crying, but I don't know why. I didn't take any pills that would make me cry. I cling to Nickel and he holds me in his arms.

"Trotsky," he tells me. "You're Trotsky."

Nickel is wearing the suit from the pod. Only it's not really there. My hand goes through the fabric and touches his shirt underneath.

A coffee mug floats in the darkness above me.

I go to the staff room. I buy a coffee from the vending machine and sit at the table. Someone has left an empty mug behind. It's the same mug as from the pod. When I try to pick it up, my hand goes through it.

A knife floats in the darkness above me.

I watch a news show playing on the monitor in the staff room. A reporter tells me a woman has killed her husband somewhere in the city. A police officer holds up a bloody knife in a bag. It's the knife from the pod.

I go in search of Nickel. I find him in Thatcher's cubicle, sitting on the floor and cradling Thatcher in his arms. Thatcher is naked and crying.

"Thatcher," Nickel tells him. "You're Thatcher."

"I don't think I should get in the pod again," I say.

Nickel smiles at me. He never stops smiling.

"But getting back in the pod is what you do," Nickel says. "It's what everyone does."

"You don't do it," I point out.

"We all have our own pods," Nickel says.

I don't know what he means by that, so I tell him I'm getting sick.

"I see things that aren't there," I say. "I'm hallucinating, and not in any good way."

"What you're feeling is very common," Nickel tells me. "It happens to everyone."

"Did it happen to you?" I ask.

"I'm management," Nickel says. I don't know what he means by that either.

"It looks very promising from my end," he adds.

Thatcher gets up and wanders off, still naked, in the direction of the staff room. "I am not here," Thatcher says. "I am not here." He walks past me like he doesn't even see me.

"We'll just adjust the programming and you'll be as good as new," Nickel tells me.

I worry maybe I'm dying. Maybe it's radiation from the pod. Maybe I've had a tumour all my life, growing slowly in my brain. Maybe it's sick building syndrome. I saw a show online about that once.

Toxic mould in the air ducts.

Old asbestos inside the walls and ceiling.

Viruses unique to the office's ecosystem.

The show said everyone dies a little more each day just because of their workplaces.

I've been sick at work all my life. But the symptoms keep changing, so I can't tell what's really wrong with me.

The first time was in university. I was halfway through my first year at the downtown campus. All my classes were in an underground complex with no windows. There were rumours it had once been a jail. I hadn't made any friends. My parents never came to visit me. The only people I talked to were clerks in stores and strangers in chat rooms online.

I didn't know what to major in, so I took the usual intro courses: psychology, economics, film studies, marketing, biology. I didn't even know why I was in university. I just didn't know what else to do. Then I went to a job fair held in a grocery store that had gone out of business. I met a woman dressed in urban camouflage at one of the booths. She hired me to work for her company, A Beta of One. A viral marketer. They couriered me products I was supposed to use in crowded areas, like food courts and nightclubs, so other people would want them.

A new energy drink.

New running shoes.

New headphones.

Every one of them made me sick.

The energy drink made me nervous for hours after I drank it. I had to take two sleeping pills just to get back to feeling normal.

The running shoes made the skin on my feet blister and peel. I had to buy bandages to cover my feet.

The headphones made me feel dizzy whenever I wore them. I kept falling down, until I bought earplugs to put in while wearing the headphones.

I recorded all the side effects on the feedback forms that came in the envelopes and sent them back to the company, and the company kept sending me new products. I used so many products, I developed a sense of what they were going to do to me before I even took them out of the courier packages.

A canister of a new body spray. The chemicals in it would give me minor burns after a few hours. I bought an antiseptic cream to treat the burns.

A new phone. It would give me headaches after only a few minutes of use. I bought extra Tylenol.

A new coffee drink in a can. It would keep me up for a day and then I'd collapse into unconsciousness wherever I was when its effects wore off. I bought more bandages for the cuts I'd receive when I fell.

Maybe I could have stopped using the products, but I never tried. I needed the money, but that wasn't the main reason. The more products I got, the more I wanted. I couldn't help myself from checking off the feedback forms' boxes that told A Beta of One to send me new shipments. I dropped out of my classes and spent all my time using products in the campus food courts and libraries and shops.

Then the university newspaper posted a special report revealing A Beta of One wasn't a viral marketer at all. It was a product-testing company disguised as a viral marketer. The report called its employees lab rats. The newspaper said two students had died, one from a reaction to a new T-shirt and the other from eating a new chocolate bar.

I didn't care. I couldn't help myself. I checked off the boxes to send me more products.

But the packages stopped arriving after the report came out. I didn't know what to do next. It was too late in the semester to enrol in my classes again. And I had bills to pay. I had things to buy. I went into the mall and found a placement agency.

The placement officer I saw was a woman with an artificial hand and a name tag that said Vegas. She asked me some questions about A Beta of One and what sort of things I liked to do. I told her I liked to spend time in the mall. I told her I liked to have money so I could buy things in the mall. She said she had the perfect job for me.

She sent me to work as a professional shopper for a stealth company located in an old factory building. It had a price for a name: $3.141. Other companies hired it to generate demand for their products. I worked there for a couple of years, on purchasing campaigns to increase the online profile of companies. I sat at a table in a long row of tables. There were still pieces of old factory equipment scattered throughout the building, but nobody knew what any of them did. There were hundreds of people like me, working on computers tethered to our tables with locks so we wouldn't steal them. A daily email told me which products to buy.

A new eyeliner.

A do-it-yourself dildo kit.

An instruction manual on how to make fake driver's licences.

I used the credit card number and address supplied by the company for the purchases. The address was the same as the office, but I never saw any deliveries. I didn't know what happened to the products after I ordered them. But I couldn't buy enough of them.

I never went back to university.

Some of my co-workers told me $3.141 had other offices that generated negative publicity about companies. They said these offices had staff who made up rumours about sweatshop fires, harmful chemicals in products' manufacturing processes, outsourced jobs. My co-workers told me you could hire $3.141 to destroy your competitors. My co-workers told me sometimes $3.141 was targeting the same companies it was working for.

People came and went all around me. There were different faces at my table every day. I stayed longer than anyone else. I never knew what happened to the others who disappeared. Some time after I started at $3.141—a year, maybe?—I had to play characters while doing my job. The daily email said it was important for job satisfaction that I believe in what I was doing. The email said I would do a better job and be more productive if I believed I was the sort of person who would actually order the products I did. The email said it would help me believe by telling me who I was.

I started having blackouts as soon as I began playing the characters.

The daily email told me to buy a pair of dress shoes. It told me I was a customer service representative for a bank and my old ones had worn out. It said my feet hurt so much, I was limping by the end of the day.

I came to after a few hours and discovered I'd been browsing online auction sites. I'd ordered a pair of combat boots worn by a marine killed in Iraq. Then I'd bought the dress shoes.

The daily email told me to buy some aftershave. It told me I was a clerk in a menswear store. It said I had problems with self-esteem and the aftershave made me feel more confident.

I came to after a few hours and discovered I'd been browsing more auctions. I'd ordered a T-shirt worn by an undercover cop shot to death during a drug raid. Then I'd ordered the aftershave.

The daily email told me to buy some hubcaps. It told me I was a taxi driver. It said I believed I'd get more fares with newer, better hubcaps.

I came to at the end of my shift in my car, clinging to a woman sitting in the passenger seat. It took me a few seconds to recognize her as a co-worker a few computers over from me.

She looked around, blinking, but didn't seem to recognize me. All she said before going to her own car was "Not again."

The next day when I logged in to my computer I discovered I'd been browsing auction sites and ordered a pair of blood-stained pants worn by a paramedic run over by a truck. I hadn't bought the hubcaps.

I entered my own address for the shipping addresses on all the extra products I ordered.

I didn't know why I blacked out or why I ordered all these things worn by dead people. I mentioned it to a doctor the company brought in to give us all drug tests. We were in the wash-room together. He was watching me try to pee into a plastic bottle. I couldn't go because I knew I was going to fail the test, or maybe because he was watching me. He said he had to watch us to make sure we hadn't brought in clean samples and weren't using fake penises. I asked him where you could get a fake penis, but he just shook his head.

"Where can't you get a fake penis?" he said.

I told him about my blackouts. I told him about ordering the clothes of dead people online. He didn't take his eyes off my penis.

"Sounds like there's something wrong with you," he said.

"What do you think it could be?" I asked.

"If I had to guess, I'd say it has something to do with your head," he told me. "But I'm not that kind of doctor."

I couldn't pee until he gave me a pill from another plastic bottle he kept in his pocket. I didn't say anything else to him about my problems. But I did look up fake penises online. They were all bigger than mine.

I never did understand why I blacked out or why I ordered things not specified in the email. It didn't matter. The products never arrived. The woman who sat a few computers over never looked at me again. And then the daily email told me the company wasn't renewing my contract. The email said the company was switching to a software program that emulated people better than people could. The email said not to take it personally. The email said another program would write me a reference if I needed it. I asked the people sitting around me if they'd received the same email, but I was the only one.

I went back to the placement agency. This time the placement officer had a whole prosthetic arm where she used to have only the prosthetic hand. I asked her what was wrong with her.

She told me it was some sort of disease. She said it was consuming her. She said the doctors didn't know what was causing it. She said she was going broke paying for new body parts.

I asked her if it was contagious and told her about the blackouts and the products I ordered for myself.

She said she had the perfect job for me and sent me to Adsenses.

I try deep-breathing exercises at the beginning of my shift to help me focus. I learn about them from a video I watch online when I search "What is wrong with me?" There are thousands of hits, but the top one tells me the deep-breathing exercises are all I need. It says the exercises will help me find my inner self again. I think maybe that's my problem: I don't have an inner self. There are hundreds of comments from people who say the exercises helped them with their anxiety attacks, their bipolar disorders, their lives of poverty. But the exercises don't help me take control of my visions in the pod. And they don't stop the hallucinations.

A purse floats in the darkness above me.

I imagine the purse on the shoulder of a woman walking through the mall. I try to imagine myself at her side, but instead I imagine a man taller than me. More muscular. Wearing clothes I know I'll never be able to afford.

Sunglasses float in the darkness above me.

I try to imagine myself wearing the sunglasses but I can't. I imagine them on the man instead.

A black convertible floats in the darkness above me.

I imagine it parked on the side of a street. I try to imagine myself behind the wheel but can't. The car remains empty.

I go down into the mall after work and see a pair of Liquor

Tyme clerks cleaning up a broken display window. The display is empty, the bottles inside gone. Someone has spray-painted the word Resist! on the back wall. Just like the shark at the artificial lake.

I'm staring at the word, trying to understand what it means, when the woman with the purse walks past me. The woman I saw in the pod. She's alone—the man I saw with her is nowhere in sight. I reach out for her but my hand goes through the purse, through her.

I forget about the broken window and the spray-painted word and follow her through the crowd. She steps into an elevator and the doors close before I can get in. I watch the display to see where she exits, then take another elevator to that stop. It's a parking garage. I walk out into it and look around, and then she drives past, in the convertible. The man I saw in the pod is behind the wheel, the sunglasses on his head. Neither one of them look at me.

I reach out to touch the convertible as it passes but my hand goes right through it. I lose my balance and fall to my knees on the ground. They drive away and disappear in the parking garage, leaving me alone with all the empty cars.

I think maybe I can get better if I just stop imagining products for a while. The next time I get in the pod, I close my eyes and ignore the holograms. I try to think of nothing at all. I try to imagine myself back at the beach, only without the shark.

"What do you think you're doing?" Nickel's voice. In my head.

I open my eyes. I'm in darkness. No ads at all. I suddenly have trouble breathing. I don't know what to say.

Nickel is silent for a moment, and I think maybe I imagined his voice. Then he says, "What do you want?"

"What do you mean?" I ask.

"What do you want?" he says again.

I don't know what I want, so I don't say anything.

He sighs. "I used to be like you once," he says. "But then I was saved."

I try to push myself out of the pod. The door is still locked.

"It was like there was this sudden light inside me," Nickel says. "I saw what I was missing. I saw what everyone was missing."

I wonder if I'm hallucinating all of this. I close my eyes and try to think of nothing again.

"Do you know what you're missing?" Nickel asks me.

"I don't know," I say.

"A motto," Nickel says.

"A motto," I say.

"Do you have one?" Nickel asks me.

I don't think I have a motto, but I'm not really sure.

"A motto is the meaning of life," Nickel says.

"What's your motto?" I ask him.

"I'm in charge," Nickel says.

"I see," I say, although I really don't.

"You need to find a motto," Nickel says, "before a motto finds you."

Nickel takes everyone in the office on a corporate retreat for the day. We go to Gun World, an indoor shooting environment in the mall. It has theme ranges, where you can shoot at video targets projected on the walls, and a special counter where you can rent all the guns from the latest movies. At the checkout, Nickel tells us we can shoot as many people as we want but the company is paying for the first three clips of ammo only.

I rent a handgun that the clerk tells me is the hottest thing in all the music videos right now, and then I go into the Inner City Warfare range. Reagan's already there. He's got an assault rifle. The video on the other wall shows a bank robbery in progress. Cops hide behind parked cars while gunmen in body armour drag hostages down the street. I didn't know you could rent assault rifles. Now I want an assault rifle.

Reagan sprays the wall on full-auto, emptying his clip without aiming. The screen flashes red where the bullets hit people.

"You're killing innocent people," I point out.

"What do you mean, 'innocent'?" Reagan asks, reloading.

"You know, people like us," I say.

Reagan just looks at me and then empties the new clip into a taxi full of screaming women.

I consider going back to the rental counter to exchange the handgun for an assault rifle, but the video might be over by the time I return. I settle for shooting at people watching the street battle from office windows overhead, but I can't seem to hit any of them.

"There's something I've been meaning to ask you," I say to Reagan.

He reloads again and opens fire on a traffic helicopter. "I wish I could do this in real life," he says.

"They'd kill you," I say.

He just nods.

"What do you think I'm worth?" I ask him.

He looks at me and then back at his gun. "I'm not really sure where you're going with this," he says, "but I'm not interested in workplace relationships."

"I meant insurance-wise," I say. "Isn't that what you did in your old job? Figured out what people were worth?"

Reagan looks for a new clip in his bag on the floor, but it's empty now. He sighs. "It depends on how you die," he says.

"How do most people die?" I ask him.

On the screen, a gunman executes a man in a suit and tie with a shot to the back of the head.

"Let's say you're on your way to the office," Reagan says. "You take a revolving door in the mall. Only your tie gets caught in the frame as you exit. A faulty seal on the door. We later find out mall maintenance is aware of the problem but has done nothing to repair it. The door spins at high speed as the woman behind you is rushing through. She's late for work. Your head is jerked to the side. Your neck is broken."

"Do people really die like that?" I ask.

"Every day," Reagan says.

"That's tragic," I say.

"That's a statistic," Reagan says.

I shake my head. "Never mind. So what am I worth?"

"I'd say a million dollars base for the incident," Reagan says. "Not too hard to get given the negligence."

"I'm a millionaire," I say. I fire several shots at a woman in a business suit trying to hide behind a flower stand. The screen finally flashes red for me. She keeps shrieking after I shoot her, but I don't care. I know I've killed her. I can kill them all. I'm in charge here.

"It's a quick death," Reagan says, "which is unfortunate. If you'd burned or died in some other way where people had to listen to you scream, then you could have earned double that. Suffering always pays."

"Still, a million dollars," I say.

"Do you have family?" Reagan asks. "A wife? Kids? Anything?"

"There's no one," I say. I fire more shots at a UPS driver running from a building to his truck and the screen flashes red again. The UPS driver gets into the truck and drives off anyway.

"Do you do anything charitable?" Reagan asks. "Coach baseball? Feed AIDS victims on their deathbeds? Help blind people get home?"

"This is it," I say, gesturing at the shooting range.

"So what we see at work is what we get," Reagan says.

"A million dollars," I say again. I shoot the woman behind the flower stand some more.

"Break it down," Reagan says. "That works out to around fifty thousand a year over a standard twenty-year career."

"I could live on that," I say.

"You're dead," Reagan reminds me. "Anyway, statistics indicate most men live about a decade after their career life, so the number's more like thirty-three thousand and change. Which works out to about twenty-seven hundred a month. Let's say seven hundred a week. A hundred a day. Four dollars and change an hour. Seven cents a minute. A little over a cent every ten seconds. Almost nothing a second."

I consider the math and don't say anything. I try to shoot a man with headphones who comes out of a Starbucks without seeming to notice the mayhem on the street. But the handgun is out of ammo.

Reagan reaches down for a shell casing on the floor.

"This is it," he says, holding up the casing. "This is what your life is worth."

I try to go home after Gun World but I can't get to my apartment. When the elevator from the mall opens in my building's lobby, the way is blocked by police tape. I move to go under it, but a cop on the other side pushes me back. She tells me they're investigating a bomb threat. She tells me I'll have to find somewhere else to sleep tonight.

I don't want to spend the money on a hotel, so I go back to work. It's late when I get there, and everyone else has left. I strip and put my clothes in the recycling basket. I put the recycling basket in the control room. I push myself into the pod. I can't sleep. I imagine products floating in the darkness above me. I imagine better versions of me using them. I lie there until Nickel pulls me out in the morning.

"How long have you been here?" Nickel asks me.

"It feels like all my life," I tell him.

He takes me to the staff room. I don't bother getting dressed because it's almost time for me to start working for real. He buys me a coffee from the vending machine. On the monitor, an oil rig somewhere shoots a geyser of flame into the sky. I reach for the mouse on the table to find some other show, but the mouse is just another hallucination. I try not to cry.

"I don't know what's wrong with me," I say, "but whatever it is, it's getting worse."

Nickel looks at the spot on the table where I reached for the mouse, then at me. "It's an occupational hazard," he says, handing me the coffee. "Like carpal tunnel and post-traumatic stress."

"So it happens to other people?" I ask. "It's not just me?"

"It's everyone," Nickel says. "Your mind prefers what it sees in the pod. Something to do with pleasure centres. It's trying to make what you imagine real."

"I'm like an addict," I say.

"Exactly," Nickel says. "Only a good kind of addict."

"How do I make it stop?" I ask.

"We haven't entirely figured that out yet," he admits. "But some people can keep it in check by buying real products."

"Real products?" I ask.

"From stores," he says.

"Does the company cover that?" I ask.

"We only cover expenses for officially recognized syndromes," Nickel says.

On my lunch break I shop in the mall. I buy inexpensive things: magazines, a box of plastic forks, random products from the shelves of a dollar store. Back in the office, everything I see seems to actually be there. I throw everything I bought in the staff room garbage, but Nickel walks past at that moment and tells me it can all be recycled.

He pulls a magazine from the garbage.

"This could be turned into memo paper," he says.

A water bottle.

"A stir stick."

A Frisbee.

"A credit card."

I reach for the mouse. This time it's there. I wake the monitor from sleep mode. It plays a video about a suicide bombing in a grocery store somewhere. Fragments of people sit on the shelves.

A hand.

A piece of scalp.

A foot still in a Nike running shoe.

Nickel pulls out a package of nails.

"Shrapnel," I suggest.

Nickel is right: real products make me feel better. I buy things in the mall every day and the hallucinations fade. I take the purchases back to my apartment instead of throwing them out somewhere Nickel can find them.

A stapler.

A set of martini glasses.

An empty photo frame.

I put them on shelves and tables where I can always see them.

A plant stand.

A pedicure kit.

Another empty photo frame.

The only photos I have in my apartment are of my parents. I need the photos to remember what they look like.

My father's been dead for years. The last time I saw him was when I helped pack all my mother's things into boxes that he put in their building's garbage room. When we were done, we stood in the condo and looked at the empty spaces on the walls where pictures had hung, the empty spaces on the floor where furniture had been. He put out his hands for a moment as if he were holding her, then dropped them. I knew I was supposed to say something to comfort him—that's what people do in the movies when things like that happen—but I couldn't think of any words. I put my hand on his shoulder but he just shrugged it off.

"You're no different," he told me. When I asked him what he meant, he just shook his head. He never said another word to me. That night, he took every pill in his medicine cabinet and overdosed. I maxed out my credit cards to pay for the deluxe funeral service, the one where you hire extra people to grieve during the service, to make it look like he had more friends and family than he did. My mother didn't come to the service. Maybe I should have hired someone to play her, too.

I don't know if my mother is still alive or not. She changed her name when she joined the commune, and my father wouldn't tell me her new name. She hasn't tried to get in touch with me since, and I don't really expect her to. She was always forgetting me.

Once, she lost me in the mall on the way to meet my father. I remember holding her hand and then, when I looked up, I was holding the hand of a mannequin. A security guard found me there, crying and clinging to the mannequin, and took me to the lost and found. The clerk made several announcements over the PA system. A woman I'd never seen before tried to claim me. The clerk asked her for ID and the woman offered to pay for me instead. The clerk was thinking it over when my parents wandered up, carrying bags of things they'd bought. When the clerk asked where they'd been, my mother said she knew where I was because of the announcements, so they went on with their shopping. I watched my father stare after the other woman as she disappeared back into the crowd.

My mother gave me things from her bags to stop my crying. All I can remember of them now is something shiny and red, something I could see my reflection in, something that pricked my finger and drew blood. I remember sucking on a price tag. I remember my mother turning the bag inside out to show me there was nothing more inside. I remember my father giving money to the clerk.

I think about his last words all the time, but I still don't know what they mean.

If I don't have photos of my parents to look at, I remember them as faceless people. Mannequins.

I feel almost normal after buying all the products. I don't forget who I am or cry for no reason. I still hate the sight of myself, and wish I were the men from my visions in the pod, but I figure I'm making progress. I imagine this is what life could be like all the time.

But all that changes after a few weeks, when Nickel doubles the amount of products we see in the pods. He says it's the economy. He says only we can find the products that can save us. He still smiles all the time, but now sometimes he bites his lips when he does it.

The products fast-forward in the darkness above me.

A pair of ballistic sunglasses.

I'm a drug lord, standing in a factory watching people process cocaine for me. Bodyguards stand at my side.

A handgun.

I'm a cop, pulling over a car for a traffic stop. When I open the car's trunk, I find a gym bag full of cash. I tell the driver I won't report him if he doesn't report me. I take the gym bag back to my car as he drives off. There's too much money to even count.

A lighter.

I'm a restaurant owner, pouring an olive oil bottle full of gasoline into a garbage can in the restaurant kitchen after everyone else has gone home. I light it and watch the flames rise up, until they reach the ceiling. I think about the insurance money.

A bottle of wine a metal vase a set of weights.

I forget who I am again when Nickel pulls me from the pod. And I hallucinate things everywhere.

I reach for a frozen dinner in my freezer, but it's not really there.

I reach for a shirt in my wardrobe, but it's not really there.

I try to buy a coffee in a Starbucks in the mall, but the Starbucks isn't really there.

I start having blackouts again. I come to and find myself wandering around stores without any memories of how I got there.

I tell Nickel about it when I'm stripping for the pod. I'm afraid to touch anything in the room because I'm not sure what's real and what's a hallucination.

Nickel just nods. "Your condition is developing an immunity," he says. "Like those superbugs in hospitals. You have to hit it with something more powerful."

"Like what?" I ask.

"More expensive products," he says, pushing me into the pod.

I shop until my credit cards are maxed out.

I buy a pair of Oakley sunglasses.

I buy a Herman Miller office chair.

I buy a package of the most expensive condoms I can find.

I apply for higher limits on my credit cards.

The hallucinations fade again.

I remember who I am again.

But I worry about what will happen when my condition, whatever it is, develops an immunity to the expensive products. I decide I need a new job, one that won't make me sick. If such a job exists.

I go back to the placement agency and update my profile on one of the computers and then wait in the waiting room. All the seats are taken, so I stand underneath the monitor on the wall and watch live video of a jet circling an airport with jammed landing gear. I don't see how it ends because Vegas comes out to get me. She has a bandage over one of her ears now. I wonder if they make prosthetic ears.

Back in her cubicle, I tell her I want a new job.

She pulls up my profile on her computer. "You haven't been at the Adsenses job that long," she says.

"It's making me sick," I tell her. "So sick I don't even know what's wrong with me."

She looks at her computer and shakes her head. "Your psychological profile says this is the right job for you," she says. "So does your credit record."

"I'm hallucinating," I say. "I see things that aren't there."

"That's part of your job description," she points out.

"I hallucinate when I'm not supposed to hallucinate," I say.

"That sounds like dedication to me," she says.

"I want a different job," I say.

"What kind of job?" she asks.

"Something real," I say.

"What do you mean, 'real'?" she asks.

"You know, construction or something like that," I say.

"Where I make real things. I think it's all this imaginary stuff that's making me sick."

"Those jobs don't really exist anymore," she says. "Besides, you haven't even made it through the probationary period yet. We'd have to give them a refund."

"A refund for what?" I ask.

"A refund for you," she says.

I know I can't keep on buying products forever to make myself feel better. I'll run out of money and credit eventually. I don't want to imagine what will happen then. I try to think of other ways to get products, but the only thing I can come up with is stealing them from stores. If I don't have to pay, I can fill my apartment with them, as many as it takes to never get sick or have hallucinations again.

I've never shoplifted before, so I go online to learn how it's done. I watch security footage of people dropping things into bags, down their pants, into fake babies in baby carriers. I practise in my apartment with the things I've bought.

I go to the Liquor Tyme and browse the aisles. I stay out of the line of sight of the security cameras. When all the clerks are busy dealing with a man screaming about his declined credit card at the cash register, I take a bottle of champagne from a shelf and slip it into a bag I bought just for this. I don't know if it's a good brand or not, but it's expensive. I walk out of the store.

A man in a Liquor Tyme shirt and bow tie steps out of an aisle near the exit and grabs me by the arm, pulling me back into the store. I try to break free, but he twists my arm around behind me and just like that I don't have control of my body anymore. He moves me where he wants me, and when I resist, the pain is what I imagine being hit by a Taser must feel like.

"I don't understand," I say as he guides me into the back-room. "I stayed away from the cameras."

"*I* was watching," he says.

The backroom is a maze of shelves and pallets of liquor boxes. He takes me over to a conveyor belt with empty bottles moving along it. The belt goes through a hole in the wall, and for a moment I think he's going to throw me on it, and I'm going to go where all the recycling goes. But instead he grabs a bungee cord from one of the shelves and wraps it around my wrists, like handcuffs, then fastens the hooks of the cord to one of the conveyer belt's support posts. I worry he's going to call the security guards, the ones who interrogated me earlier, or maybe even the police.

"I'm sorry," I tell him. "I've never done anything like this before."

"That's what everyone says," he tells me.

"But it's true with me," I say.

He just nods. "Don't worry," he says. "You're not going to do it again."

He doesn't call the security guards or anyone else. Instead, he takes off his bow tie and sets it on one of the shelves. Then he takes the bottle of champagne from my bag and rips off the foil. He pops the cork out. He grabs my hair and pulls my head back, and I cry out at the pain.

"It's just aversion therapy," he tells me. "I took a course on it. I'm certified."

He thrusts the bottle in my mouth and the champagne flows down my throat. I have no choice but to drink it. I try not to choke but I can't help it. There's too much champagne. It runs out of my mouth and burns its way through my nose.

"It's for your own good," the man says. "You'll thank me someday." He says it like he really means it.

I gag and cough, but he doesn't take the bottle away, not until it's empty. When he finally lets go of me, I bend over and try to catch my breath, then vomit on the floor. He walks away, leaving me alone. I look around at the shelves of wine cases, the empty bottles passing me by on the conveyer belt, the fluorescent lights overhead, and try not to cry.

He comes back with a mop and pail. He takes off the bungee cords and watches me as he puts his bow tie back on.

"Clean it up," he says.

I'm too afraid of him to run. I clean up my vomit as best I can. While I work I see there's more of it on my shirt and pants, but there's little I can do about that.

When I'm done, he nods and grabs me by the arm again. This time he leads me to one of the cash registers. He puts the empty champagne bottle down and the clerk there looks at it, at me, then runs it through without changing expression. I pay for it with one of my credit cards. I shake a little when the transaction is approved. The clerk puts the empty bottle in a bag and hands it to me. The man with the bow tie walks me out into the mall. He shakes his head.

"That's a waste of a good champagne," he says.

I walk away from him as quickly as I can, heading off into the mall.

"Please come again," he calls after me.

I wonder if Nickel is right, if a motto is all I need to make me feel better. I lie in bed awake all night trying to come up with one. I can't sleep after the Liquor Tyme incident anyway. Every time I close my eyes I see the clerk stepping out from behind an aisle for me.

The next day, as I'm getting ready for the pod, I tell Nickel I've come up with a motto.

"I am what I buy," I say. It's the only thing I could come up with.

He smiles at me for a long minute, but it's a smile that doesn't reach his eyes.

"That's the motto for the Born Again Consumers group," he says.

"Who are they?" I ask, but he just shakes his head.

"You have to come up with your own motto," he says. "You can't just take other people's mottos."

"What difference does it make?" I ask.

"The difference is trademark infringement," he says. "We don't need to get sued for what you're thinking."

I spend the night trying to come up with more mottos.

The world is what I make it.

I look it up online. It's the motto of an architecture firm.

You're no different.

The motto of a repossession agency.

I need help.

The motto of an addiction-counselling franchise.

My mind is full of other people's mottos. Whatever I think up, it's owned by someone else.

I worry that none of my thoughts are actually mine.

I call in sick to work, but I'm not really sick. I just want a break from the pod. I need to empty my mind.

I go to an oxygen café in the mall and relax on the patio. The wall behind me is painted to look like a street in Europe somewhere, with the Eiffel Tower and Big Ben in the background. A monitor over the Coliseum plays *Panoptical,* a news show about the day's worst disasters in the city. It's hosted by a woman named Paris. She wears the kind of jackets and necklaces you see only on news shows. She tells me about bombs that have been going off in city buses, and shows me footage of the carnage. Burning vehicles, people screaming and cops pointing their guns at the camera. I take deep breaths from an Ocean Breeze puffer and wonder if this is what the ocean really smells like.

The man at the table next to me breathes from his own puffer while scrolling through messages on his phone. He has a product I've seen in the pod. A tattoo of the World Trade Center in flames on one of his arms. I worry for a moment that maybe I'm hallucinating him, that he's just another vision, but the man with the tattoo I imagined in the pod was younger, with a shaved head. A game developer who drove a Lexus.

When this man leaves, I reach over for his discarded puffer. It's real. French Delight. I take a sniff of it. Cigarettes and espresso.

Paris shows me close-ups of charred bodies still sitting in their seats on the buses.

"Remember," she says, "it could happen to you."

I leave Paris and her disasters behind and follow the man into the mall. I stop him outside a PharmaWorld by grabbing onto his arm, his tattoo. He's real, too. When he turns to look at me, I ask him where he got the tattoo.

He shakes his head and says something to me in a language I don't understand. I wonder if it's French.

He breaks free of me and goes into the PharmaWorld. I keep following him. I wander the aisles after him. Whatever he puts in his basket, I put in mine. He looks at me every now and then and shakes his head some more, but that's it.

I don't know what else to do. Buying the things he does is as close as I can come to the life I imagined in the pod.

I stand in line behind him at the checkout. The woman who rings in my purchases doesn't seem to notice they're the same as his. By the time she's done, he's disappeared into the mall. I look for him for a few minutes, but he's gone. I go home with the products instead. I lay them out on my bed and look at them.

Shaving cream.

Razor.

Shampoo.

Conditioner.

Condoms.

People magazine.

I try to imagine what he's doing with his products right now. I undress and take the shampoo and conditioner into the shower. I wash my hair. I use the conditioner. It's a lemon scent I'm not used to. I feel like a different man.

I get out of the shower and towel off. I shave with the new razor and shaving cream.

I go back into the bedroom. I put on one of the condoms.

I look at the people in the *People*.

I masturbate.

I sleep.

I start seeing products from the pod everywhere. Real products. I think maybe Nickel was right after all. Maybe I am powerful.

I see a cop in a grocery store wearing glasses from the pod. I follow him like I followed the man with the tattoo, buying everything he does in the store. A bag of pasta. A jar of spaghetti sauce. A block of Parmesan cheese. I brush my basket against his in the frozen-food aisle to make sure he's real. I make my dinner that night and think of him out there somewhere, eating the same dinner. I wonder what he's thinking about.

I see a man on the news interviewed about gun crime in the city. He's wearing a tie with angels on it. I saw the tie in the pod. He's holding an envelope he's about to drop in a mailbox. I freeze the image and zoom in on the envelope, record his return address. I buy a box of envelopes and mail them all to his address. I leave them empty. I don't know what to give him. But I feel closer to him by sending the envelopes. I can almost imagine touching his tie. I can almost imagine his life.

I see a man in a dollar store cutting products with a box cutter from the pod. I watch from the ends of aisles as he slices open a package of licorice and takes one, slices open a juice box and drinks from it, slices open a package of condoms and drops one in his pocket.

I follow him out of the store, into the mall. He goes up a

nearby escalator and into a multiplex cinema. I keep following him. I buy a ticket for the same movie he does. I sit behind him in the cinema, which is almost empty.

When the lights go down, he jumps over the seat and onto my lap. He holds the box cutter to my throat. It's real.

"What do you want?" he asks me.

I look around for help, but the other people in the cinema just watch us. On the screen, a car drives along the streets of a city.

"What do you want?" he asks again.

"Where did you get it?" I ask him.

"Get what?" he says.

"The box cutter," I say.

The car comes to a lineup of other cars and stops.

"Are you a cop?" he asks. "Mall security?"

"Can I buy it from you?" I ask.

"Why?"

"I'm not really sure," I say.

There's an explosion. When the flames and smoke fade, all the other vehicles are crumpled, scorched shells along the side of the street. The first car is untouched, its metal and glass still gleaming. It drives on.

"It's mine," the other man says and slashes my face with the box cutter.

The mall has its own emergency rooms. I go to one and wait an hour before anyone sees me. Everyone else in the waiting room has bags from different stores. I try to imagine the products in them. I wonder if there's anything from the pod.

I watch an ad on the monitor hanging from the ceiling. The camera moves over a suburban neighbourhood of houses with green lawns and paved driveways, then swoops down to a young couple entering one of the houses. The people are real but the houses all look CGI.

The image fades into a caption.

HomeBrand.

If You Don't Live Here, You Don't Live.

Now Under Construction.

A nurse takes me to a room full of beds separated by curtains. I lie on one of the beds and close my eyes. It's just like the pod, except for the sound of someone vomiting nearby.

After a while, an intern comes into the examining room. His eyes are red. He sips from a Starbucks cup while he looks at me.

"So what's wrong with you?" he asks.

I point to my cut. "I just want to know if it's real," I say.

He comes over and pokes the cut a little, and it bleeds some more even though it doesn't hurt. My face has gone numb for some reason.

THE WARHOL GANG 61

"It's real," he says. "Did you do that to yourself?"

"I think I'm dying," I say and tell him about the hallucinations.

He just nods and sips some more, then checks my blood pressure. He listens to my heart, my lungs, my stomach. He shines a light in my eyes. He puts on a latex glove and feels around inside me.

"This must be what it's like when the aliens abduct people," I say.

"Try not to breathe," he says. He seals my wound with a bandage and some cream. When he's done, he tells me there's nothing else wrong with me.

"But I see things that aren't there," I point out.

"Let me clarify that," he says. "You're no worse off than anyone else who comes in here."

So I tell him about how buying products makes me feel better. I tell him about following people in the mall. I tell him I think that if I can find the right products, I can be a better man. I tell him I can't help myself.

He listens to it all and then shrugs.

"Maybe the aliens put something in you," he says.

At work the next day, Nickel asks what happened to my face.

"It was an accident," I say. He nods and pushes me into the pod without saying anything else.

That afternoon, we hold our first terror drill. In the memo he sends around, Nickel says the terror drills will make us better people by making us appreciate our lives more. You have to own your fears, the memo says. I think that's a motto but I'm not certain.

The first one is a fire drill. Nickel runs around the office yelling "Inferno!" and tossing orange pieces of confetti onto desks and people. He even opens the pods and throws confetti inside.

"How did it get in here?" I ask him, climbing out of my pod.

"This is a fire escape drill," Nickel says, "not a fire detection drill."

"What about the sprinklers?" I ask, pointing at the ceiling. "How come they're not putting out the fire?"

Nickel points at some confetti on my shoulder. "Are you going to do something?" he asks. "Or are you just going to stand there and burn?"

I get dressed and take the elevator down to the mall. The thought of dying in a fire makes me want to buy things. The Club Escape video shows a scene of hot-air balloons now. When I walk into the elevator, it's like stepping into the sky.

I wander around the mall until I find myself in a spy-gear store. I look at miniature cameras that can be hidden in stuffed animals. I look at special lights that reveal semen and blood stains invisible to normal eyesight. I look at a police scanner. A man with a scar on his forehead and a name tag that says Resist! comes over and tells me I can use the scanner to listen to whatever I want.

"The police, the fire department, the ambulances," the man says. "That's the beginner stuff. With the right add-ons, you can listen to phone conversations, to baby monitors."

The man's name tag makes me nervous. It reminds me of the Liquor Tyme, and the out-of-control shark at the beach. I want to ask him about it, to see if it's some sort of viral marketing thing, but I'm too distracted by the scanner. I've seen it before. In the pod.

I remember static coming from it. I remember I was a cop, standing with other cops and looking at something on the ground. An outline of a body. I lay my hands on the scanner. It's real. I lift it from the shelf.

"Air traffic controllers," the man goes on. "Security guards on their walkie-talkies. If you get a portable scanner, you can listen to fast-food people. You can disconnect someone else's phone if you're close enough and know the right tricks. You can do whatever you want."

I take the scanner to the register at the front of the store. When the clerk there asks if anyone helped me with the purchase, I look for the man with the scar. I don't see him anywhere.

"His name tag said Resist," I say.

"We don't wear name tags," the clerk says.

I wonder if I hallucinated the man. On the way back to work, I keep touching the scanner in its bag to reassure myself it's real.

There's a sticky note on the door of my pod. It says the elevator became stuck between floors as a result of the fire. It says I've been incinerated. It says never to take the elevator in a fire situation. It says most fire deaths in office towers are caused by elevator failures.

It doesn't say how I'm supposed to save myself.

I take the scanner home. I set it up in my living room. I listen to it while making dinner and watching shows on the monitor in the kitchen. I mute the shows so that all the dialogue comes from the scanner.

10–10 at 323 Avenue, a woman talking about the stock market says.

10–34 at the King Street McDonald's, two hockey players shout while punching each other in the head.

I find an index of scanner codes online and memorize them while eating.

10–51 in the Queen area, a reporter says on a dark street. Roaming gang.

10–23 at the airport, a pregnant woman tells a man, folding her arms across her chest. Bomb threat.

I can't stop touching the scanner. It's real. It's all real.

I tell Nickel about the scanner the next day at work, while I'm taking off my clothes before getting into the pod.

"I imagined it and now it exists," I say.

He hugs me and this close I can smell his body odour, feel the sweat on his back through his shirt. I never imagined him as someone who sweats.

"Now do that to everything you see," he says and locks me in the pod.

The scanner changes my world.

After work, I go home and turn on the scanner again and hear a call about a man run down by a car at an abortion clinic. The address is only a couple of blocks away. I can see the accident for real.

I take the elevator back downstairs but instead of descending into the mall I get out in my building's lobby and go through the doors that lead to the street. It's the first time I've been outside in weeks. I run to the clinic. Before I'm even halfway there, I'm coughing from the exhaust of all the vehicles stuck in traffic. The air's not as clean as inside the mall.

I get to the accident scene before the paramedics do. The victim lies underneath the car, which is still parked in the entrance of the lot. Abortion protesters kneel around the car and the injured man, laying their hands on both and murmuring words I can't make out. Homemade signs with pictures of bloody fetuses litter the ground in a circle around the car. The driver's still inside, shaking her head at the whole scene.

"I'm not even pregnant," she yells out the window.

"Shame!" a few of the protesters call out.

"I was just trying to turn around," she says.

I watch the circle of praying people until the sound of sirens gets louder. Then one of the protesters grabs me and drags me down to kneel beside the car. At first I think she wants me to help her try to move the car. But instead she forces me to lay my hands on the victim along with everyone else.

I feel the heat of his skin.

I feel his heartbeat.

I feel his blood on my hands.

I've never felt anything so real in my life.

The paramedics arrive and pull me away to make room for them, but I know it's too late. I can tell from the look the trapped man gives me that he knows he's dead.

I can't stop thinking about that moment I had with him.

I think about it the next time I climb into the pod and wait for the ads to start.

A handful of vitamins shaped like Jesus float in the darkness above me.

I imagine myself in a kitchen I don't recognize. A woman gives me a Jesus vitamin and a glass of water. I take the vitamin and drink the water. The woman kisses me, and then some children—

a young boy and girl—run into the room. They take their own vitamins and hug me. We sit down for breakfast together. We hold hands as we pray.

A pair of dress shoes float in the darkness above me.

I put on the dress shoes and a jacket and kiss my family goodbye. I go out the door to a car with men waiting in it. Some of the protesters from the abortion clinic. We drive to the clinic and meet the rest of the protesters. We stand in a circle and pray and hold hands. I can feel the warmth of their hands in mine, the warmth of their love. These people are my family, too. I take a sign of a bloody fetus like the rest of them. I look for the man who got run over but don't see him.

A car floats in the darkness above me.

I imagine myself lying under the car at the abortion clinic. I realize I'm the victim. I can't breathe. When I try to talk, nothing comes out of my mouth but blood. I lie there, and everyone kneels around me and lays their hands on me.

I'm dying, but I'm not alone.

When Nickel pulls me from the pod and holds me in his arms, I'm crying, but it's not the same as before. I'm not bewildered or confused. I don't feel hollow inside. I can still feel the hands of the protesters on me. I can still feel their love. It takes me a moment to recognize what I'm feeling.

I'm happy.

I can't sleep at night. I can't stop listening to the scanner, even when I'm in bed. I lie in the dark and watch the mall's spotlights sweep over my building, turning my apartment into an X-ray of itself. I can see the cobwebs on the ceiling, the fingerprints on the windows from the previous tenants. I listen to the calls for help. I can't stop thinking about the man from the abortion clinic, all the other men like him out there. All their friends and families crying for them, praying for them.

I go to work and lie in the pod. I imagine myself as the man at the abortion clinic over and over.

A bottle of champagne floats in the darkness above me.

I celebrate my wedding anniversary with my wife. We go for dinner at a restaurant. We leave the kids with babysitters. We spend the night in a hotel room. We make love overlooking the city.

A soccer ball floats in the darkness above me.

I watch our kids play soccer and baseball. I watch them graduate from high school. I watch them bring home dates.

A car floats in the darkness above me.

I go to work. I sell cars. The lot is full of the cars I've seen in the pod. I sell enough of them that I can buy a car from the pod for myself.

Every product I see that day, I imagine more and more of the dead man's life. I'm not sure why his life doesn't fade away like all the others. Maybe because the memory of him is so strong. Maybe because he was real.

The love I have for his life doesn't fade away when I get out of the pod.

I go home and imagine I'm still him. I make extra portions when I prepare dinner, for the family. I set extra places at the table. At night, when I try to sleep listening to the scanner, I imagine his wife beside me.

But all that changes when Nickel increases the rate of the ads again. When he calls us into the meeting room to announce this, I notice he hasn't shaved, and he has bags under his eyes. But he's still smiling.

"The economy depends on you to save it," he tells us. "The world depends on you to save it."

Now the ads flash in the darkness above me so fast I can't concentrate on anything. I try to imagine myself in the house, with my wife and kids, but I can't.

A red pillow a soap dispenser a keychain drive.

I try to imagine myself at my job but can't.

An empty envelope a set of blinds a black notebook.

I try to imagine myself back under the car at the abortion clinic but can't.

An electric fan a silver alarm clock a red courier bag.

I close my eyes but the products burn through my eyelids.

When Nickel lets me out for a break, I throw up in an empty recycling bin he's placed beside the pod. I can hear Nader and Reagan and Thatcher throwing up in their cubicles, too.

"You need to slow down the ads," I say.

"We need to make quota," Nickel says.

I know I have to find something real to fix me again. I get dressed and go down into the mall. But this time the mall doesn't make me feel any better.

I see the dead man from the abortion clinic, the man I've been for days, in the window of a Banana Republic store. He's a mannequin. He's still bleeding and looking around for help, but now he's wearing dress jeans and a black sweater. He gives me the same look he gave me when he was trapped under the car.

I know he's just a hallucination but I run anyway. I don't go back to the pod. I go home. I listen to the scanner. I know what's happening. An immunity. I know what I have to do. I have to go to another accident scene.

I go out to the first call I hear.

I drive to a Home Depot. Firefighters stand around the entrance, looking down at a part of the store's sign that has fallen from the building and onto someone. They talk about whether or not they should order the crane. They talk about their budget. They've blocked off the area with yellow tape but left a pathway so people can still get into the store.

The sign covers the victim so all I can see is a bloody hand sticking out from underneath it. I crouch down and hold the hand. It's still warm. I try to imagine the victim under the sign, but before I can, a firefighter yells at me to get away from there.

I go inside the store. I grab products at random from the shelves to make it look like I'm just another shopper. A drill gun, a roll of duct tape, a carton of light bulbs. I leave bloody fingerprints on whatever I touch.

I go back outside with my purchases to find that the firefighters have managed to lift the sign and have taken the victim away. Other firefighters are cleaning the blood from the scene with a hose. Soon it will look like nothing happened here. I go back to my car and go home. I lie in bed and try to imagine myself as the dead man under the sign, whoever he was, but I can't. I'm just me. Alone.

The next morning as I'm getting undressed for the pod, Nickel asks what happened to me the day before. He's wearing the same clothes as the mannequin in the window of the Banana Republic.

"Nothing," I say. "Nothing happened to me."

"Find your motto," Nickel says, shaking his head and pushing me into the pod.

I watch more disasters on *Panoptical*. I want to find out how to act like I belong at accident scenes. I don't want to get chased away from a victim again.

Paris shows me a commuter plane that went down in a sewage pond. Men in boats pluck the remains from the water.

Plastic foam cups.

A volleyball.

A teddy bear with a price tag still attached.

The men in the boats all wear the same black jackets. They put everything in evidence bags and write notes on them with felt markers.

"Remember," Paris says, "it could happen to you."

I listen to the scanner. A woman in a motorized wheelchair is crossing a street when the battery on her wheelchair dies and she's hit by a bus.

I drive to the scene and park behind a transit official's car. I remember the men in the boats and the jackets they wore. I take a transit jacket from the back seat of the other car and put it on.

The paramedics work on the woman, who lies amid a mess of broken jars and dented cans from her torn grocery bags. I can't get near her, so I find the bus driver instead. He's sitting on one of the handicapped seats on his bus, weeping. I sit beside him and put my arm around him.

"Tell me what happened," I say.

But he doesn't say anything, just looks out the window and watches the paramedics carry the woman away. When a police officer climbs into the bus to interview the driver, I get back in my car and go home. I take the jacket and some of the dented cans with me.

Paris shows me a clip of a man and woman leaping hand in hand out the window of a burning bank tower. The people who take away the bodies photograph them first.

I listen to the scanner. A homeless man in a dumpster is emptied into the back of a garbage truck and impaled on a shard of broken mirror. I arrive and wave my camera at the nearest officer. She looks at me, at my transit jacket, then goes back to talking about traffic with the truck driver.

I climb into the back of the truck but someone has already taken the homeless man away. There's nothing to photograph but my own reflection in the bloody, broken mirror. I climb off the side of the truck and run away when another man with a camera gets out of a car.

Paris shows me a clip of two teens dying when they crash the car they stole from a dealership. The car hits a pole and rolls down the street, until it's just a crumpled ball of metal, then bursts into flame.

The men and women who look at the bodies afterward wear latex gloves and surgical face masks. The audio catches a man saying the car is a total write-off.

I listen to the scanner. A UPS driver is stabbed by a bicycle courier at a red light.

I arrive on the scene before the paramedics. I wear the transit jacket I took from the other accident scene. I get out of the car and put on latex gloves and a surgical face mask I bought at a PharmaWorld. I tell the cops I'm an off-duty nurse and they wave me past the tape and then go back to keeping the crowd away.

I get in the truck and kneel beside the UPS driver, who's lying on the floor amid scattered parcels. I touch him and feel the heat of his skin through the gloves. I feel his heartbeat, his blood. I hold his hand and he stares at me. It's just like the abortion clinic. I know I'm going to be all right again.

I go through the motions of the first-aid moves I saw online. I push down on the man's chest with both hands but stop when blood squirts out of the wounds and onto my gloves. I try to blow air into the man's mouth but forget I'm wearing the surgical mask. The man grabs onto me and tries to say something, but all that comes out of his mouth is more blood. When the paramedics show up, they have to pull him off me. He won't let go. One of the paramedics starts real first aid on him, while the other looks at the blood on my mask.

"Are you okay?" he asks me.

"I think I'm getting better," I tell him.

I listen to the scanner every night. I watch *Panoptical* online every night. There are hundreds of comments for each video. People talk about how they would have shot the scene, how they would have rescued the victims, how they would have died.

Paris shows me a video of a woman sitting on the ground, holding a dead boy in her arms. The boy's head is half blown away from a bullet, and her lap is bloody.

I imagine a brain scan from work, all of it dark.

Remember, it happened to you, a commenter says.

I watch the woman clean the blood from what's left of the dead boy's face. I watch her stroke his hair. I watch her bend down and kiss his shattered forehead.

I wonder what it would be like to have someone care for me like that.

I mark the video as a favourite.

I go out to accident scenes with my transit jacket and other props every night. I hold the victims in my arms as they bleed and choke and cry out for help. I leave the scenes whenever the real emergency personnel arrive, before anyone starts asking questions of me. I take whatever I can from the victims.

I slide rings off their fingers and wear the ones that fit.

I pick up their glasses from the ground and spend a day or two wearing them, seeing how the victims saw the world.

I pull their phones from their pockets and put them in mine. I call their friends and families. I pretend to be the victims for as long as I can. I ask these other people where they are and what they're doing. I ask them when I'm going to see them next. Sometimes they already know the person I'm pretending to be is dead and they ask me who I am. They ask me why I'm doing this. I listen to them weep. I wish I could be there with them to take them into my arms. To comfort them.

The victims' things make me feel better than the products I buy from stores. I don't get dizzy. I don't hallucinate. My fantasies about living their lives last longer when I have something to remember them by.

But it all fades away after a while, just like everything else. I get in the pod and can't imagine myself as the UPS driver anymore. I get in the pod and can't imagine myself as the taxi driver crushed by the dump truck that lost its load. I get in the pod and can't imagine myself as the doctor burned to death by the bomb left on his doorstep. It's just me, lying there naked and alone, looking at things that aren't real and may never be real. Trying to remember lives I can't live.

I start taking the keys of victims at accident scenes. I go to their homes. I want to learn as much as I can about them. To help my fantasies last even longer.

I sit on their couches and lie on their beds. I turn on their computers and go through their web histories. I look at their photo albums. I look at them with their friends and family. I look at them eating dinner with other people, skiing with other people, dancing with other people.

I look at them holding other people.

This is it.

This is what I want.

I want their friends.

I want their photo albums.

I want their lives.

I make meals with their food and eat with their dishes.

I put on clothes from their closets.

I look at their photos and imagine myself in them.

I am loved.

I've found my motto.

I am not alone.

Nickel takes everyone in the office to a retreat at the same cinema complex where the man with the box cutter slashed me. Nickel tells us we can watch whatever movie we want, but we have to pay for our own snacks.

I go into a cinema with Nader and Reagan and Thatcher. I think I should feel nervous, should be looking around for the man who cut me, but instead I feel calm. Maybe because of my motto.

The ads for the other films don't stop. I feel a sudden need to buy something. I go out to the lobby and get the biggest drink they have and a package of licorice. I hear applause from a different cinema and go into that one to see what movie is playing.

Only it's not a movie. The cinema is one of the bigger ones, with seats for what must be a thousand people. The screen shows a man in a suit standing at a pulpit. In one corner of the screen it says Live from Las Vegas. In the opposite corner it says People Saved. The number goes up as I watch.

The man on the screen looks at me. "You've done a lot of things wrong," he says in a voice so loud I can feel it vibrate through me. "But it's okay to forgive yourself for those things."

I think I'd like to forgive myself, only I'm not sure what I've done wrong.

The screen divides into windows showing dozens of other cinemas. Thousands of people stare out from the screen at me.

The people around me raise their arms in the air and whisper words I don't understand. The people on the screen do the same. I wonder what's happening.

Then a spotlight illuminates a section of the stage in front of the screen. There's a lineup of people there. Then spotlights turn on in all the other cinemas.

The man is still in the screen, in a window in the middle now. His voice is just as loud. "Confess your sins and be forgiven," he says, and a woman steps into the spotlight on the stage.

"I steal clothes," she says into a microphone. "I try on outfits in stores and just walk out. I leave my old clothes in the change rooms."

The people around me close their eyes and bow their heads. They murmur to themselves. I eat my licorice.

A man steps into one of the spotlights on the screen. "I tell my wife I sleep with women on business trips," he says. "But it's a lie. I never sleep with anyone."

Another man steps into another spotlight on the screen. "I steal my neighbour's mail. I've tried to stop, but his life is just so much better than mine."

I find myself going down to join the line. I don't know what I'm going to say, but I want to stand in the light. I want everyone to pray for me.

But there are maybe a hundred people in the line, and the light is turned off long before I'm anywhere near the stage.

The man fills the screen again, looking down at me. "Remember," he says, "we'll be watching."

The screen goes blank, leaving us all in darkness for a few

seconds. Then the house lights come up and people start filing out of the cinema. Others stay in their seats, heads bowed.

I sit down in a nearby seat and look up at the blank screen. I try to pray but I don't know what to pray for. I still don't know when the ushers cleaning up the cinema tell me I have to leave.

I spend more and more time in the apartments of victims I know have died. I listen at their doors first to see if anyone else lives there. Sometimes I hear people talking inside, or crying. When that happens I put my head against the door to try to hear what they're saying, but I can never make out the words. When neighbours step out of their apartments I just walk away down the hall, like I belong there.

But when I don't hear any voices I go inside and spend whole days and nights in the apartments. I eat what's left of the victims' food and sleep in their beds. Take baths in their tubs. Shit in their toilets. I live their lives instead of my own.

I take some of their photos home and put them up around my apartment. I take one of the few photos I have of myself and make dozens of copies. I buy cheap frames from the Ikea website. I put the photos of myself in the victims' apartments, in the places of the ones I took, so it looks like I belong there.

I don't worry about anyone coming home during all of this. They're dead, after all.

But then a woman does come home while I'm in one of the apartments, and I have to hide.

I took the keys to the place from a motorcycle rider who was ripped in half when his bike hit a light post. The man's upper body flew through the air and lodged itself in the middle of an abandoned billboard. People stopped their cars and bicycles and took photos of it. His lower body wound up underneath a Coca-Cola delivery truck parked in front of a convenience store. I found it before the paramedics and cops because they were taking photos of the billboard, too. I couldn't believe his legs and lower body were real until I touched them. Still wearing his motorcycle leathers. It looked like some sort of medical mannequin.

I took the man's wallet as well as the keys. I wanted to see what I could buy with his credit card.

I saw the woman's clothes in the apartment's closet, saw the photos of her on the bookshelf. But there were dirty dishes in the sink and the plants were all dead, so I thought maybe they'd broken up. Women never leave dead plants around. The first time I visited, I loaded the dishes into the dishwasher. When I came back, they were still in the dishwasher, untouched. The plants were still dead. That's when I figured I had the place to myself.

I'm standing in the living room, adjusting the photo of myself on the bookshelf, when I hear the key in the lock. For a moment I think it's the man come home, that he's somehow survived, that the surgeons have put him back together. I dive behind the couch.

But it's not the man—it's the woman from the photos in his place. I watch her in a mirror over the faux fireplace. She drops her keys on the table by the door, where I've put his keys—mine now—and looks around.

"Hello?" she calls. She pulls a suitcase through the door and then I understand. She's been away. Travelling. She's not calling to me. She's calling to the dead man. Only she doesn't know yet he's dead.

I close my eyes and imagine I'm the dead man riding home on my motorcycle at this very moment, as she goes into the kitchen and makes herself a cup of tea and opens the mail she's brought in with her. While the tea steeps, she goes down the hall to the bathroom and has a shower.

I get up from behind the couch. I think I should leave before the woman notices some sign of me. But then I see the mail she's left on the kitchen counter and I can't help myself. I go over to it.

An invitation to a wedding and a credit card statement in the dead man's name. I look at the list of purchases and try to imagine what he bought.

A charge from a liquor store.

A bottle of wine for a dinner with the woman.

A charge from a jewellery store.

An engagement ring for the woman.

A charge from a motorcycle shop.

The helmet I was wearing when I was killed.

I go down the hall and watch the woman move behind the shower curtain. Then I go into the bedroom.

It's the same Ikea bed as mine, only larger. The same Ikea laundry basket, only the clothes inside it are different. It's been easy to imagine myself as the dead man. But now the woman's pants and underwear and shirt sit at the top of the laundry. She turns off the shower. I slip into the closet, past the clothes on hangers and into the back. I haven't been this deep in the closet yet. There's a row of hooks on the wall here, with things hanging from them. Handcuffs. A whip. A blindfold. A rubber gun. I run my hands over them. I stop shaking as soon as I touch them. I didn't know I was shaking until then.

She comes into the bedroom wearing a towel. I watch from inside the closet. She drops the towel on the laundry basket and puts on pyjamas she pulls from the dresser. The same Ikea dresser as mine. She goes into the kitchen and comes back with her tea and a magazine. She climbs into bed and reads, sipping the tea every now and then. She looks at the clock on the bedside table and sighs.

I can smell her on the clothes in the closet. I want to change into the victim's clothes. My clothes. I want to reach out and touch her.

She falls asleep reading. I wait for what feels like an hour. When her breathing is deep and regular, I leave the closet, watching and listening with each step. I stop beside the bed and look down at her. I touch the sleeve of her pyjamas. She's real. I'm not imagining her. I wish I could imagine what she's dreaming.

I turn out the light and take the wedding invitation with me. I leave behind my photo.

I go out to a call at an auto show in the convention centre. A woman dressed like an angel—white bikini and fake wings—to promote a set of new tire rims is burned when a booth's pyrotechnics go off and ignite her feathers. When I get there, the paramedics are discussing the best way to load her onto the stretcher. The wings have melted into her skin in places. Men in shirts and ties cluster around, filming her with their phones, as she looks around for some way out of what's happened.

She meets my gaze and doesn't look away. I step out of the crowd and kneel beside her, take her hand. And that's when my life changes, although I don't know it yet. The paramedics look at me in my transit jacket and face mask and latex gloves, and they try to pry me free but she won't let go. They shrug at each other and let me in the back of the ambulance with her. They swear when they see someone has spray-painted Resist! on the side of the ambulance.

We race through the streets to the hospital. Cars pull over to make room for us, and pedestrians wait to cross the street until we've passed.

"I wish I was you," I tell the paramedic who sits in the back with the burned woman and me.

"I wish you were me, too," the paramedic says.

I slip off the woman's ring when he isn't looking. But she sees it.

"You're going to be all right," I tell her to distract her from what I've just done.

"I don't think so," the paramedic says.

I've never been with a victim this long. I squeeze her hand. I think I should say something to her. I try to think of what I would want someone to say to me if I were in her position.

We come to the hospital and the paramedics push me out of the way. They take her out of the ambulance and roll her toward the emergency room doors. I tell her the only thing I can think of.

"You are not alone," I call after her.

She raises her hand in what I think is a wave, but then she wiggles her ring finger and winks at me.

I don't know who she is, but she's not like the other victims. And then she's gone.

I go back to the apartment where I watched the woman. Miriam. That was the name on the wedding invitation. Miriam and Anthony. Anthony. The motorcyclist. The dead man. Me. I go back to the closet and wait for her to return home. I test out the things on the hooks to pass the time. I run the whip over my back. I consider putting on the handcuffs but I worry I'll get trapped in them. I twirl the gun on my finger, put the end in my mouth.

Just like that, I imagine our lives together.

I imagine Miriam as an admin assistant for an office supplies company. I imagine living in the apartment with her for real.

I imagine cooking dinner with her.

I imagine watching *Panoptical* with her.

I imagine fucking her handcuffed on the bed.

Only it's not her. It's the woman from the ambulance.

I hear the door open and wait for Miriam to come into the bedroom. Instead, I hear a man's voice.

"Hello?" he says. "Is anyone home?"

For a second I think I must be hallucinating again. I know it can't be Anthony. I don't know who it is. I bite down on the gun. It's real.

I hear the man in the kitchen, opening cupboards and moving things around, and I head for the door. I'll run past the other man, whoever he is. I'll distract him by dropping my wallet. Anthony's wallet.

I look around the corner, into the kitchen. It's a mailman.

He's wearing a postal uniform and has a postal bag slung off one shoulder. His back is to me. He takes a bottle of wine from the wine rack and drops it in his bag. Then he does the same with the coffee grinder on the counter.

I go past the kitchen and press myself against the living room wall. I listen to him go down the hall, into the bedroom. I follow him. I watch him empty dresser drawers onto the floor, then drop a jewellery box into the bag. When he goes to open the closet door, I step into the room.

"No," I say.

The mailman spins around and stares at me.

"I didn't think you were home," he says.

"I'm not," I say. "Not really."

He looks at the gun in my hand.

"I'll put it all back," he says.

He puts the jewellery box back on the dresser. He picks up the clothes from the floor and shoves them back in their drawers.

"I don't normally do this," he says, looking at me.

"Neither do I," I say.

That's when we hear someone at the door.

I push him into the closet. There's barely room for both of us. This close, I can smell his sweat. He looks at me and then feels the gun. He shakes his head as I pull the closet door nearly closed.

We hold our breath as Miriam walks into the room. She lies down on the bed without taking off her clothes. I try to think of what to say if she sees us.

It's not what you think.

He's the robber.

I was just here waiting for you.

I was just here pretending to be Anthony.

She's still for a moment, and then she begins to weep. She goes on and on, and I close my eyes and try to imagine more of our life together, but I can't with the mailman beside me.

When her crying turns into the heavy breathing of sleep, the mailman shakes his head again and steps out of the closet. He's careful not to make any noise, and she doesn't wake. The mailman goes back to the kitchen, and I follow him.

The mailman takes the knife block from the counter and puts it in his bag.

"What are you doing?" I whisper to him.

"I don't know who you are," the mailman whispers back, "but you're not who I thought you were."

I go back to the bedroom and watch Miriam some more.

I think I should call 911, but I don't know what I would say.

When the mailman leaves, I follow him out the door, but we go different directions down the street.

I can still taste the gun in my mouth.

For a week, all the ads in the pod are for vehicles. Sports cars, minivans, pickup trucks, shuttle buses—every vehicle you can imagine. I'm always the driver, but I'm a different person each time. A different victim I've encountered before.

A minivan floats in the darkness above me.

I drive the minivan through the neighbourhood I saw in the HomeBrand ad. I'm a man who crashed his car into a bus stop in the middle of the night and was thrown through the windshield. When I went to his apartment, there was mail from a law office on his kitchen counter. Divorce papers. On the walls were photos of him with a woman and children. There were empty bedrooms in the apartment.

A pickup truck floats in the darkness above me.

I drive the pickup to the Home Depot where the sign fell on the man. I'm a man who was killed on his way to work at a construction site by a drunk driver. His apartment was almost empty—just a mattress on the floor and some clothes in the closet—but there was a photo of a woman in his wallet.

A taxi floats in the darkness above me.

I drive the taxi around the city streets. I'm a man who was found shot to death in his car at a red light. He was wearing one of those earpiece phones. When I listened to it, there were the sounds of a woman weeping on the other end. When I went to his apartment, I listened at the door and heard the same woman weeping inside.

I imagine all these women as the same person. The burned woman in the ambulance. I can't stop thinking about her.

At the end of the week Nickel takes everyone in the office down into the mall, to one of the food courts. A space has been cleared in the middle of the food court and a platform assembled with a ramp leading up to it. On the platform is a BMW.

People sit at nearby tables, eating their meals and watching as Nickel gathers us around the platform. I'm not sure, but I think he's wearing the same clothes as the day before.

"You've all shown remarkable dedication to the company and the economy," Nickel tells us, swaying a little. "And to your mottos."

I look around the food court, at the car, at the people staring at us, at everyone but Nickel. I wonder if we're getting laid off, if this is some sort of going-away ceremony.

"You've done a lot for the company, so now the company is going to do something for you," Nickel says. "It's going to give you the chance to make your dreams come true." He points at the BMW. "And this is your dream."

We all look at the car. I try to remember if I saw this particular model in the pod. I could have, but I'm not really sure. There were so many cars.

"Research tells us this is everyone's dream," Nickel adds.

He tells us to gather around the car and lay our hands on it.

He tells us the last person still touching the car wins it.

He tells us gas and taxes are not included.

We all go up the ramp and gather around the car. There's not enough room for everyone from the office, so we push and shove each other as we try to grab hold of the car. I find myself hanging on to the passenger-side mirror, alongside some people I don't recognize. I don't see what happens to Reagan and Nader, but Thatcher stands at the driver's-side window, trying to open the door. It's locked.

Now I wonder if maybe this is an ad, if we're on one of those secret-camera commercials. I look around, but all I can see are people in the food court taking photos with their phones.

I'm the first to let go. The car makes me think about the man at the abortion clinic, and the next thing I know I'm lying under the car. The other people hanging on to the car cheer. Nickel comes over to ask me if I'm all right.

"I've never been better," I tell him.

"Then back to the pod with you," he says. He looks at the car and touches it for a moment before walking away.

Back in the office, there's no one to put me in the pod. I push myself into it anyway and think about scanner calls.

When I get out for a washroom break, Reagan and Nader are in the staff room, watching an ad for the upcoming Sniper Bowl. Men and women lie on the floor of a stadium and shoot at targets on tracks. The targets are all faceless mannequins. Corporate logos flare up over their heads when they're hit. This bull's-eye brought to you by Nike. McDonald's. FedEx.

Nader says the receptionist sprayed people with pepper spray and made half the office quit. "She had it in her purse," he says. "She pulled it out, but no one would actually let go until she started squirting them in the eyes with it." He sighs. "I had to buy a new shirt."

Reagan says the man who delivers the office mail threatened to kill him. "He even showed me his knife," he says. He shrugs. "I lost my driver's licence on an impaired last month anyway, so what the hell."

"What happened to you?" Nader asks me, but I just shake my head.

When I go home, I walk past the car. Thatcher and a dozen others still hang on. Different shoppers sit and eat their meals and watch the contestants. Thatcher stares inside the car.

I go back to the placement agency. Vegas is in a wheelchair now, a blanket over her legs, bandages over both her ears. I tell her again I want a new job. I tell her I must be out of the probationary period by now.

She looks at my records on her computer and raises her eyebrows. "Yes, but your job satisfaction scores are quite high," she says.

"What are you talking about?" I ask. "I'm not satisfied with my job."

"No, but the job is satisfied with you," she says.

"What is that supposed to mean?" I ask.

She leans back in her chair and folds her arms across her chest, the fake one over the real one.

"It means you're not going anywhere," she says.

"But I don't want to work for Adsenses anymore," I say.

"What you want doesn't matter," she says. "What the company wants matters. And the company likes you so much it's put a hiring freeze on you. We can't place you anywhere else."

"But I want to be a paramedic," I say.

"You're doing what you do best," she says.

I go back to work after the weekend and pass by the car in the mall. I'm surprised to see Thatcher and a few others still hanging on to it. Their eyes are red with exhaustion and their clothes untucked. I wonder if they're allowed washroom breaks.

Nickel calls me and Nader and Reagan into the meeting room before we start. "You all have to become Thatcher," he tells us. "We need him back on the team, and the contest is taking longer than we thought to finish."

"What do you mean, 'become Thatcher'?" I ask.

Nickel peels off my name tag and puts a new one on my chest. It says Thatcher.

"You'll take turns being him," he says. "You'll use his pod. Try to imagine how Thatcher would think."

Reagan and Nader nod, but I shake my head. "Why does someone have to be Thatcher?" I ask.

"He's on the payroll," Nickel says. "We need a work record. We need his imagination." He opens the door to signal that the meeting is over.

"But who will be me?" I ask as the others file out. No one answers.

I can't tell the difference between Thatcher's pod and mine. They're the same size, and I feel the same panic when Nickel locks me in the new pod as I do in my own pod.

But the visions are different.

An electric razor floats in the darkness above me.

I imagine myself standing in a bathroom, holding the electric razor. I imagine looking at myself in the mirror. I imagine Thatcher in the reflection.

A pillow floats in the darkness above me.

I imagine the door to the bathroom open. I imagine seeing a bedroom on the other side of the door reflected in the mirror. I imagine a woman I don't know sleeping on the bed, her head on the pillow. I imagine this must be Thatcher's wife.

A photo frame floats in the darkness above me. I try to imagine myself in it, but all I can imagine is Thatcher and the woman from the bed in a wedding photo.

When Nickel lets me out for a break, he holds me in his arms while I weep and try to remember who I am.

"Thatcher," Nickel tells me. "You're Thatcher."

I go to the staff room and find Nader already there. He's watching some business show on the monitor, but there's a new monitor on one of the other walls, streaming an episode of *Panoptical*. Paris shows me an accident at a warehouse. A forklift drives down an aisle with barrels of chemicals on its lift. A warehouse worker steps out of an intersection in the forklift's path, and the driver slams on the brakes. The barrels tumble off and to the floor, and the lid cracks open on one. The man on foot clutches at his throat and falls to the ground, writhing. The forklift driver jumps out of the vehicle and tries to run back the way he came.

I imagine myself as the forklift driver. I try to imagine getting away from the chemicals, hiding in the staff room until the firefighters come and save me, but I'm old and overweight, and there's something wrong with my right leg, so I can only limp. I gasp for breath but it's like breathing acid. My mouth and nose burn, and then my insides. I slump to my knees and claw at the shelves around me, and a stack of boxes falls on my head.

I notice Nader looking at me.

"What are you doing?" he asks.

"I'm watching *Panoptical*," I say, nodding at the monitor.

He gets up and walks over to the wall. He waves his hand through the monitor. It's just a hallucination.

"You're seeing things, aren't you?" he asks.

I get up and go to one of the vending machines. I buy a bag of chips. The new monitor fades. I hold the bag to my head to keep the hallucination away.

Nader looks at me, at the chips. "Nickel gave you his line about buying things, didn't he?" he says.

"It keeps things from getting too bad," I say. "For a while, anyway."

He shakes his head.

"What you need is something real, all right," he says. "Something *really* real."

After work, Nader takes me to Social.

Social is a club in the basement of one of the bank towers downtown. The entrance is a door at the end of a deserted hallway and looks like it leads to a trash room, or maybe a loading dock. There's no sign, just a security camera over the door.

"Act like you belong," Nader says, looking up at the camera.

"Belong to what?" I ask.

"Anything you want," Nader says.

But when I look up at the camera, all I can think of is the security guards who questioned me. I'm ready to turn around and run when the door opens.

"It's a private club," Nader says as he leads me inside. "That way no one can get sued."

"Sued for what?" I ask, but Nader shakes his head.

"We're not supposed to talk about that anymore," he says.

Social looks like any other lounge in the basement of a bank tower. The members look like bankers and clerks and accountants. They sip drinks at tables and watch the monitors on the walls. I don't see why it's so special it deserves the camera and secret entrance.

We sit at the bar and order beer and watch the monitors. One of them shows market updates, another shows a different commercial for HomeBrand. It's the same CGI house I saw before in a neighbourhood of CGI houses just like it. The couple from the first commercial step into the house. It's empty inside, but then furniture appears in every room they enter. They walk into the living room and a couch and chairs appear. They walk into the kitchen and a new refrigerator and stove appear. They walk into one of the bedrooms and a young boy appears.

"I used the buyout money from my last job to get a membership here," Nader tells me as we drink our beer. "That's why I'm working with people like you instead of sitting on a beach somewhere."

"I'm not sure that's what I would have done with the money," I say. I don't look away from the commercial.

The images fade to white and the caption appears on the screen again.

HomeBrand.

If You Don't Live Here, You Don't Live.

I suddenly realize I want to live at HomeBrand. I want the couch and stove and the young boy. I want photos on the walls of me and my friends. I want the life of the people in the commercial. I feel it so badly that I order another beer to fill the emptiness inside me.

"It was the best investment I ever made," Nader says, looking around the room.

We drink in silence for a moment, and then Nader nods at the bartender and leads me into the back of Social, into a long hallway lined with doors.

"If you could be anybody else, who would you be?" Nader asks me. He opens doors to show me the rooms behind them.

An office with a couple of cubicles and computers and filing cabinets.

A room with bleachers against one wall and a video screen showing a basketball game covering the opposite wall.

A room made to look like a bus stop, complete with a bench and bus sign, the floor painted to look like a road. There are even fallen leaves around the bench.

A room made to look like a hallway in the mall. All the walls are video screens, showing stores and people wandering along with bags. A lone bench and garbage can occupy the centre of the room.

I have no idea what's going on.

"This is on my tab," Nader says. "Whatever happens, try to remember that." He leaves me in the fake mall.

I sit down and wait, even though I don't know what I'm waiting for. I watch people walk in and out of stores on the video screens. I drink my beer.

After a moment she walks in the door and sits on the bench beside me. She's carrying a shopping bag and she looks inside it for something while I stare at her.

It's the burned woman from the ambulance. Only her hair is a different colour, and she's wearing glasses now. But it's her. I'd never forget her. I can't even stop thinking about her. I pull aside her shirt and jacket to check. I see the burn scars on her back from the melted wings. And dozens of other scars.

She straightens up and pushes me away. "What are you doing?" she asks.

"I know you," I say.

She looks at me a moment and then smiles. Raises her hand and wiggles her ring finger.

"What's going on?" I ask. I look around for cameras. I wonder if I'm on some sort of reality show.

"That depends," she says. "What would you like?"

When I look back at her, she's pulled a knife from her bag. It's the same knife I saw in the pod, the same knife I saw on the news when the woman killed her husband.

"Where did you get that?" I ask.

She shrugs. "Somewhere in the mall," she says. She grabs my shirt and pulls me closer. She runs the tip of the knife down the scar on my cheek where the man in the cinema slashed me. The knife is real.

My mouth turns dry and my heart pounds at the touch of the metal on my skin. But I also feel myself getting an erection.

"I'm going to assume you want the regular," she says. She reaches into my pocket and pulls out my wallet. She goes through it one-handed, taking out my cash and credit cards. She looks at my Adsenses pass card. She digs the knife into my cheek, pushing me off the bench and onto my knees. Then she empties the shopping bag on the floor—silk scarves, the price tags still attached—and shoves it over my head.

I don't understand what she's doing until she wraps the ends of the bag tight around my neck. Then I drop my beer glass and try to tear the bag off, but I can't get my fingers underneath the edges. I roll on the floor, trying to get away from her, but she rolls with me, holding me in her arms. I gasp for breath and suck the bag into my nose and mouth. Then I can't breathe at all and I black out.

I come to with the bag still on my head, although it's loose now. I think for a moment I'm still in the pod and I wait for the ads to start. Then I remember where I am and I pull the bag from my face and sit up.

People keep walking in and out of stores on the video screens around me, but she's gone.

I go back out to the bar. Nader watches me with a smile. He's ordered another beer for me. When I sit down, he slides me my wallet. I open it and see everything is there: my cash, my credit cards, my Adsenses pass card.

"That was fast," Nader says. "I guess it really was your first time."

I don't know what to say. I look at myself in the mirror behind the bar. It's only then I see I cut my arm on the broken beer glass during the struggle. My shirt is covered in blood. I still have an erection.

"Who is she?" I ask Nader.

He grabs a menu from a rack and flips it open. There are several pages of photos showing the rooms in the back. Dozens of rooms. At the end of the menu are a few pages of head shots. Men and women smiling at the camera. Nader points at one of them. It's her. A single word under her photo.

Holiday.

"She's an actor," Nader says. "They're all actors."

"An actor," I say.

"No need to thank me," Nader says.

The next day at work I can't stop thinking about Holiday. It's still my turn to be Thatcher, and I keep imagining myself as him. Only now I'm Thatcher living my life.

A set of tire rims float in the darkness above me.

I'm back at the convention centre where I first encountered Holiday. She's lying on the ground, smoking, the wings melted into her. She writhes and cries in pain.

A phone floats in the darkness above me.

Men press in from all sides around me, filming Holiday with their phones. She looks at them and stops crying. She smiles at me.

A man's wedding band floats in the darkness above me.

Holiday raises her hand like she's waving to me and then wiggles her ring finger.

When Nickel lets me out of the pod, I don't want to be alone, so I follow him as he lets Reagan out of his pod and then tries to take out Nader. But there's something wrong with Nader's pod and Nickel can't open the door. Reagan and I lean against the pod, naked, while Nickel pulls on the handle with both hands and mutters to himself. Mottos, I imagine. I think about Holiday and her scars some more. I think about the auto show where I met her. I ask Reagan if he ever met anyone who faked accidents when he worked as an insurance agent.

"Every claim I ever had was fake," Reagan says. "Even the real ones."

"I don't understand," I tell him.

"Everybody makes stuff up," Reagan says. "I lost my priceless collection of first-edition comics in the fire, along with all the receipts to prove I bought them. I hurt my back in the crash, not before. I must have got AIDS from a blood transfusion, because I'm a married man."

"But do people make up the entire accident?" I ask.

Reagan looks at me, then back at Nickel working on the door of the pod. "I had a family once," he says. "Everyone had cancer."

"You were married?" I say. I had no idea.

"It wasn't my family," Reagan says. "It was a claim."

"A whole family with cancer?" I ask. "What are the odds?"

"They gave it to themselves," Reagan says. "They said they got the cancer because the house was too close to power lines. It was. You could feel it in the air. There was some sort of leak or something. It would power the lights when they weren't even turned on. It scrambled the images on their computers. Their phones wouldn't work. It was like the place was haunted."

Nickel hammers on the door and Nader screams from inside.

"They sued our client," Reagan says. "But the kid already had cancer when they moved there. I checked his medical records. I checked all their medical records."

"What gave it to him?" I ask.

Reagan shrugs. "It was just one of those things. They didn't know who to sue. So they moved to the house and said it was the power lines."

"But you caught them," I say.

"I approved the claim," Reagan says. "They all had cancer."

"I don't understand," I say.

"The parents got cancer after they moved to the house," Reagan says. "The problem with the power lines was real. So I approved the claim. They made a story up about the kid, but it turned out to be true."

Nickel finally manages to open the door and pulls Nader out. Nader gasps for air. He's weeping.

"Thatcher," Nickel tells him. "You're Thatcher."

"I'm Thatcher," I say.

"Sorry," Nickel says, shaking his head. "Nader," he tells Nader. "You're Nader."

"So what happened?" I ask.

"My supervisor overruled me," Reagan says. "She said the case was fraud. She said three cases of cancer like that was an act of God. She said the company would fight it until the family all died, because it would be cheaper. Then she fired me for approving the claim."

"I meant what happened to the family?" I say.

"I have no idea," Reagan says.

"I'm not sure, but I may have seen God that time," Nader says.

I want to ask what God looks like, but then Nickel speaks.

"That's exactly what we're looking for," he tells Nader.

I listen to the scanner that night. I need another accident. I need an accident I know is real.

I go out to a call of a woman hit by a FedEx truck. She's sitting in the middle of the intersection when I arrive, holding a bundle of tissues to her head. The tissues are all bloody, and there's more blood on her clothes. Ripped bags lie on the ground around her, their contents spilled on the pavement.

A container of milk.

Cans of soup.

Yogourt.

I feel something inside me when I see it's not Holiday. I can't tell if it's relief or disappointment.

The FedEx driver is arguing with a cop at the front of the truck. Every now and then the woman yells obscenities at him.

I take advantage of the cop's distraction to go over to the woman. I slip off my transit jacket and put it around her shoulders.

"You're going to be all right," I tell her. "You're not alone."

She stares at me. "What?" she asks. "What are you saying?"

But then the cop comes over and grabs me by the arm and pulls me to the side.

"I know what you're doing," he says. His name tag says Flint. He keeps a hand on his gun.

"I've seen you before," he goes on. "At the shooting by the

Chinese embassy, when you pretended to be one of those Falun Gong people. At the heart attack in the McDonald's, when you pretended to be a doctor."

I wonder if what I've done is illegal.

Flint shakes his head.

"You can do better," he tells me.

Flint tells me he'll take me to all the accident scenes I want. Flint tells me he'll take me to all the accident scenes I can imagine.

Flint says I just have to do one thing for him.

He gives me street directions to an industrial park. I drive there and find all the buildings abandoned. The broken windows have For Lease signs in them, but the signs are old and faded. I park in an empty lot with a line of electricity towers running through it. The lot is just packed dirt with old plastic bags and other garbage embedded in it. I remember what Reagan told me about the family with cancer.

The lot is bordered on the far side by the highways and their off-ramps. The power lines go across the highway and disappear. I've never been across the highway. That's where the suburbs are, somewhere. I wonder if I'm anywhere near HomeBrand.

A police car pulls into the lot a few minutes after I park. Flint. He's alone, just like before. We get out of our cars and meet in our crossed headlights. The air out here smells just like it does everywhere in the city. Stale exhaust. I look around but don't see anyone else. There's a camera on the dash of Flint's car.

"Take off your clothes," Flint says. He unbuttons his shirt.

"Just what exactly is this thing you want me to do?" I ask.

"Put on my uniform," he says. He tosses me his shirt.

I hold the shirt and watch him undress for a moment. The

power lines hum overhead. Then I strip down to my underwear. He has a gun, after all.

He finishes undressing and stands there naked. He looks at me. "Everything," he says. "I need everything for this to work."

I'm not sure where he's going with this but I take off my underwear. It's not that different from work.

I put on his uniform. It's warm and damp. I can smell him. I can almost imagine what it's like to be him. He puts on my clothes and then helps me put on the holster. I take out the gun and look at it. It's heavy in my hand. I feel like I did back at Gun World, when I was shooting people.

"Don't get any ideas," Flint says. "I loaded it with blanks before I came over here." He helps me into the bulletproof vest. When we're done, he shakes his head at me and whistles.

"It's like looking in a mirror," he says.

He tells me to get behind the wheel of his car.

"You're me," he says. "I'm you. You just pulled me over."

"So I'm arresting myself?" I ask.

"You're arresting me," Flint says.

"But that's me," I point out.

"You don't exist anymore," Flint says.

"All right," I say. I know that feeling.

Flint points at the camera on the cruiser's dash. "When you get out, make sure you stay in the frame."

"What have I pulled you over for?" I ask.

"Suspicion," Flint says.

"Suspicion of what?" I ask.

"What have you done?" Flint asks.

I sit in the police car without answering. I look around the interior, at the switches and computer and shotgun in its rack. I wish I could take the car home with me.

Flint gets in my car and pulls it in front of the police car. "Action!" he yells out the window. I get back out of his car and walk up along the side of my car. Broken glass crunches under Flint's shoes. No, *my* shoes. I try to come up with some dialogue but forget about that when Flint gets out of the car and points a gun at me.

Flint's gun is shiny with a moulded black grip. It looks brand new.

I've seen this gun before.

I've seen this gun in the pod.

I realize Flint has staged all this so he can kill me out here for some reason. There's no one else here to see it. I think maybe he's some sort of serial killer who meets his victims at accident scenes.

I feel light-headed as I watch myself draw the gun and open fire. Like an out-of-body experience. But I may as well be back at Gun World. Flint doesn't drop, doesn't even flinch as I shoot at him. Blanks.

Then Flint shoots me with his gun and I'm slammed back into my body. Hammers knocking into my chest. Can't breathe. Can't brace my fall. Something hits the back of my head and I fade into the darkness of the pod for a moment.

Flint brings me back by kicking me in the side, in the legs, in the head. I still can't breathe right. I lunge up at him but he shoves me back down with a foot on my chest, pinning me to the ground.

I punch at his legs and bite him through the fabric of his pants, but he doesn't pay any attention. He aims the gun at my head.

"How does it feel?" he asks.

I stop fighting and stare at him. At the gun. My heart is pounding so fast I'm worried about a heart attack.

"How does it feel?" he asks again.

"How does what feel?" I manage to say. I can't look away from the gun.

"How does it feel to be dead?" he asks.

But I don't feel dead. I think the ribs in my chest are broken, but I don't feel the pain. I feel the rush of adrenalin instead. Like when Holiday choked me, but amplified a hundred times. Everything around me is in sharp focus. I'm aware of every piece of garbage on the ground around me. I feel every rock sticking into my arms and legs. I feel blood oozing out of the back of my head with each heartbeat. I've never felt so alive.

I think maybe he's going to shoot me again, only this time not in the vest.

"Please," I say.

"What?" he says.

I don't want this feeling to fade.

"I want to live," I say.

Flint smiles at me. He puts the gun back in his pocket.

"That was fucking *real*," he says.

He steps off me and goes back to the police car to check the camera.

"That went pretty well," he says. "I don't think we need another take."

I try to sit up, but my limbs keep spasming. Dark spots flash in my vision. Little black holes that start to grow. My heart is fluttering instead of pounding now.

"There's something wrong with you," I say when Flint comes back and offers me his hand.

"I feel better already," Flint says. "Everything wrong with me, I got it all out now."

"No, I mean there's something wrong with *you*," I say, nodding at myself. "You can't move."

Flint calls an ambulance on his cellphone. "Don't you really die on me," he says. "I can't even imagine the paperwork for this."

The paramedics who show up are the same ones who took Holiday and me to the hospital from the auto show, but they don't recognize me.

"It's a cop," the driver says to his partner when he sees me. "Better call it in."

"No, I'm the cop," Flint says. "He's just wearing my uniform." He takes his ID from a pocket on the shirt I'm wearing and shows it to them.

The paramedics look at the ID and look at each other, but don't call it in. Flint strips the uniform off me and then they load me onto a stretcher and into the back of the ambulance. Flint tosses my clothes—my real clothes—in after me before they shut the door.

"I'll call you," he says, putting his uniform back on. "We'll do this again sometime."

The paramedics take me to the hospital. They drive with the siren on and the lights flashing. Shocks of pain run through me every time they hit a bump in the road. I can't stop tasting my own blood. I think I finally understand how all those victims at accident scenes felt as they died.

"What kind of game were you guys playing?" the paramedic in the back asks me.

"That was no game," I tell him. "That was real."

"If you say so," the paramedic says.

"I think that was the realest thing of my life," I say.

"You're delirious," he says and sticks a needle in my arm.

The next day I imagine myself in the pod, and this time it's really me. Not the rich man I imagined before, the one from the penthouse condo with the expensive suit and sports car and all that. Not the man from the abortion clinic. Not all the other people I've imagined. The real me.

A toaster oven floats in the darkness above me.

I'm in my apartment. My real apartment. The toaster oven is on my counter. The counter is lined with products I've seen in the pod. I know it's really me because I see my reflection in the surface of the toaster oven. I'm naked, just like I am in the pod. Bruises on my chest, scrapes on my face. Just like in real life.

A coffee maker floats in the darkness above me.

The coffee maker is on the counter also. Two cups of coffee waiting in it.

A toothbrush floats in the darkness above me.

Holiday walks around the corner and into the kitchen. She's brushing her teeth with the toothbrush. She's naked, too. She has scars everywhere but her face.

Nickel pulls me from the pod and says the scans look good.

"You must have found your motto," he says.

He doesn't say anything about the bruises on my body from Flint's bullets, the marks on my legs and face and neck from Flint's boots.

I go to the washroom and look at myself in the mirror. I don't hate the sight of myself like I used to when I got out of the pod. I feel like I did when I first imagined the man from the abortion clinic. Happy.

Something has definitely changed.

I feel real.

Fucking real.

Reagan comes into the washroom and stares at himself in the mirror. He's wearing a name tag that says Thatcher. He doesn't say anything about my injuries either.

"You should see what I'm hallucinating today," he says and makes a sound between a sob and a laugh.

I stop by the car contest after work. It's just down to Thatcher, two other men and a woman. I don't know the others, and I wonder if they're actually people from our office or if they're people from the mall who snuck into the contest. But when I go over to talk to Thatcher, a security guard gets up from one of the food court tables, where he's filming the scene with a video camera, and tells me I'm not allowed to interfere with the contestants. So I guess they're from the office.

I show the guard my Adsenses pass card and tell him I'm here to deliver a memo from management. He frowns and talks into a shoulder mike, but doesn't try to stop me when I go over to Thatcher's side.

Thatcher's eyes are red, and I can smell him from a few feet away. All the contestants' eyes are red. The others keep rubbing their faces with their free hands. The woman cries silently and the men I don't know talk to themselves. Thatcher doesn't say anything, just keeps staring inside the car. I see now there are bloody stains on all the windows. I wonder what's been happening here.

"We need you back at the office," I tell him. I don't want to play him again. But he just shakes his head.

"I'm not going back there," he says. "I'm going back to my life."

"What are you talking about?" I ask and he slaps the car. It's then that I see his hands are covered in dried blood. He's been hitting the car.

"It's the same one," he says.

"The same what?" I ask.

"The same car," he says.

I don't know what he means. I look around for help. One of the other men climbs onto the trunk of the car and waves me over.

"He keeps trying to break the windows to get inside," he says. "I think he's really hurting himself. You should take him to a doctor or something."

"Why haven't you stopped him?" I ask.

The other man shrugs. "It's one less competitor if something happens to him," he says. "Or if someone takes him to a doctor."

I go back to Thatcher. He keeps trying the door handle on the driver's side.

"The same car as what?" I ask him.

"The same one that burned me before," he says.

I look at the car. "Thatcher, this is a new car," I say.

He shakes his head. "It's the same model," he says. He slaps it again and leaves fresh blood on the window. "Everything went wrong with the car," he says. "But that's all going to change when I win it."

"What are you going to do?" I ask.

"I'm going to burn it like it burned me," he says.

He tries the door handle again. I put my hand on the car and the security guard tells me to step away.

I go home and find a sticky note on my door. It's from Flint. It says he's waiting for me downstairs. I take the elevator to the lobby and find his cruiser on the street outside my building, the lights flashing. Flint's alone inside it. He stares ahead without looking at anything, but when I go to get in the front seat he motions me into the back instead.

"What are we going to do this time?" I ask. I think if we're going to do another film, I'd like to get a camera of my own to record it.

He doesn't answer, just drives us to one of the parking garages between my place and Adsenses. We park on the top level and look at the billboard across the street. It shows a row of naked women holding a sign in front of them. The sign advertises an upcoming fashion show somewhere. Someone has spray-painted "Fashion Is Murder" across the women's faces. I'm not sure if it's supposed to be part of the ad or not.

"What did it feel like?" Flint asks.

"What did what feel like?" I ask.

"The other night," he says.

I consider how to answer that.

"It felt like I was really dying," I say.

"It was the best thing that ever happened to me," I say.

"I want to do it again," I say.

Flint closes his eyes.

"I want another film," he says.

"All right," I say. I start to unbutton my shirt.

"A film of my wife," he says.

I pause in my undressing. "I don't have any dresses," I tell him.

"I want her dead," Flint says. "As violently as possible. Hit by a gasoline tanker dead. Raped and killed by an office co-worker dead. That would be very good for me."

"What about me?" I ask.

"I'll give you everything you want," he says.

I think about that, but I'm still not sure myself what I really want.

Flint opens his eyes again. "There must be somebody else like you out there," he says.

We look at the women on the billboard. I think again about Holiday.

"I think I may know someone," I say.

I go back to Social. I don't tell Nader. I don't want him to know about my relationship with Holiday. I don't know how I'd explain that to him. I don't even know what my relationship with Holiday is.

I look at the camera at the entrance to Social and imagine I'm Nader, lying naked in my pod. The door opens.

Social is just as crowded as before, but all of the people are different. I don't recognize any of them from my previous visit, except for the bartender. He smiles at me when I sit at the bar and order a beer.

"I knew you'd be back," he says. "You had that look when you left."

I look at my reflection in the mirror behind the bar. I can't see anything.

I flip open a menu and point to her. Holiday. I tell the bartender I want to be robbed again.

"The same room," I say. "The same knife."

The bartender shakes his head. "She's not on shift right now," he says. "She only works every few weeks. When she needs the money."

"Where can I find her, then?" I ask.

The bartender looks up at one of the monitors, at the porn

movie playing on it. Laughing women roll around a bed with a male inflatable doll.

"What makes you think I would know that?" he says.

"What do you want?" I ask him.

"What do *you* want?" he says.

"What do you mean?" I ask.

He looks at me again. "Tell me what you want," he says, "and I'll tell you where to find Holiday."

I imagine myself in the backroom again, sitting on the same mall bench. I imagine Holiday walking in and sitting beside me again. I imagine her choking me with the bag again.

The bartender studies me and then nods. He looks back at the women on the monitor. They're kissing each other now.

"Look for her at accidents," he says.

"What kind of accidents?" I ask.

"The spectacular ones," he says. "Go to the spectacular accidents and you'll find Holiday."

I go straight home after work every night. I watch videos while listening to the scanner.

Man overdosing in a McDonald's bathroom, a woman sings into a microphone.

Two men shot by each other on the street, the man doing the weather says, pointing at a smiling sun.

Woman trapped in a car wreck, a man with a chainsaw shouts.

I drive to the scene and park behind a minivan with a pizza delivery sign on its roof. I get out and put on the transit jacket and gloves. Two cops stand beside a car crashed into a street light. They look in at a woman lying in the back seat, pinned by the bent metal.

"I'm a doctor," I say and hold up my hands so they can see the gloves. I look at the woman and she looks back at me.

It's not her.

"Do something!" she screams from behind the metal.

I think about reaching into the wreck to touch her, to hold her, like I've done so many times before, but I don't. It's not the same anymore.

"Well?" one of the cops asks.

"I'm not that kind of doctor," I say and walk away.

The next day in the pod, I can't think of anything.

A pair of running shoes float in the darkness.

I can't imagine anything.

A black suit floats in the darkness.

I can't imagine anything.

A phone floats in the darkness.

I can't imagine anything.

Nickel pulls me from the pod. He shakes his head but doesn't say a word.

I go home. I sit on the couch and watch videos. I listen to the scanner.

Woman lit on fire while cooking, Donald Duck says while chasing Huey, Dewey and Louie around a room.

I drive to the woman's condo building. I wait outside the front doors until the paramedics wheel her out of the lobby. I run to her side. "I came as soon as you called," I tell her.

She looks up at me and licks her lips. Her skin is a mixture of grey and red patches, and her hair has been burned off. "Help me," she says.

It's not her.

"Are you family?" one of the paramedics asks.

"Wrong number," I say and go back to my car.

I start to hallucinate again.

A black towel on the floor of the bathroom.

A new mouse beside my computer.

A new computer.

Woman hit by a bus, a man in an ultimate fighting ring says.

I drive to the scene. Cars are lined up behind the bus, waiting for it to be moved, so I just leave my car in the traffic.

The woman is still underneath the bus, covered by a yellow

plastic sheet. Firefighters and cops stand on one side of the bus, talking to each other. I go around to the other side and crawl underneath the bus. I drag myself over to the woman and lift the sheet. Her face is gone, but I can tell from the skin colour that it's not her. I hold the woman's hand to see if I can feel any of the things I used to feel. Nothing.

Woman crashed car into a Gap, a man waiting for a kettle to boil says.

I arrive on the scene and find that the car went through the front doors of the Gap and into a crowd of mannequins after the store closed for the night. The driver's been thrown from the car. The firefighters search for her among the mannequins, ignoring the people running into the Gap to grab armfuls of jeans and shirts and socks. A man with a tattoo of a barcode on his shaved head flees with an armful of empty Gap bags and nothing else. Some of the firefighters take armfuls of clothes themselves, carrying them to their truck.

I park in the lot across the street and go over to the Gap, threading my way through the cars that have stopped so the people inside them can watch the scene. I pass by a homeless man who's come out of the lobby of the bank beside the Gap to stare at the action. Near the store's entrance, two paramedics perform CPR on an old man at a bus stop. Someone's stolen the bench seat, so they work on him on the ground. He's looking in the store, but he doesn't blink. I stand by the three of them and pretend to say a prayer. I don't actually know any prayers, so I just mutter the words from a sign in the bank's window. "We can finance your dreams," I say.

Inside the Gap, mannequins lie everywhere, their limbs tangled with metal racks. Some of the mannequins have broken open. They're hollow inside. A stack of sweaters has fallen from somewhere and landed on the hood of the crashed car, still folded. It could be one of the ads in the windows.

The firefighters find the driver of the wrecked car in the remains of a clearance table and pull her out of the store. Blood covers her face from a cut in her forehead, and her hair is streaked with different colours now, but I still recognize her. Holiday.

"The brakes went," she tells the firefighters. "I couldn't control it." She looks at the old man at the bus stop. "It was either the store or him."

The firefighters seat her on the curb and go over to help the paramedics. She faces the lineup of cars and weeps.

I grab a jacket from a rack—full price, not one of the sale ones. It sets off an alarm when I take it from the store, but no one tries to stop me. I sit beside her and drape the jacket over her shoulders.

She looks at me and laughs when she recognizes me. "We have to stop meeting like this," she says.

We watch the homeless man drag one of the mannequins into the bank lobby.

"You can do better," I tell her.

She looks around at the crash scene and smiles.

I see then that someone has spray-painted Resist! on the Gap's windows.

"What could be better than this?" she asks.

I stand in the doorway of a home-furnishings store beside an intersection, waiting for the traffic light to change. I'm wearing an army jacket. The jacket belonged to a man who got hit in the head by a truck's mirror while he was standing at another intersection. There are bloodstains on the collar.

I hold the gun Flint gave me under the army jacket. It's the same gun I used the night I pretended to be Flint. Flint gave it to me along with his wife's dress. He told me the gun's loaded with blanks again, but I'm still careful with it. I know from the videos I've watched online that even blanks can kill.

I'm wearing an Andy Warhol mask I bought in a dollar store. It covers my whole head and smells like it's giving me cancer. I try not to breathe too deeply for a while and then just give up.

Holiday was the one who found the location. I met her at a Starbucks earlier in the evening, and we drove around for most of the night, looking for the right setting, before we stopped at the intersection. We looked at the home-furnishings store beside us. A bedroom suite in the window: king-size bed, monitor on the wall, a black-and-white photograph above the bed of a woman lying dead on the crushed roof of a car. The works. A Going Out of Business banner in the window. The doors chained shut.

"Would you want any of that?" Holiday asked.

I looked at my reflection in a mirror on the wall. "I want it all," I said.

"Then this is our location," Holiday said.

The first question Holiday asked me when I told her about the film was if she would be the star. I told her that as far as I knew she would, and it was only then that she asked how much she'd get paid. I hadn't talked to Flint about that, so I told her the first number that came into my head: $3,141. She looked at me and then shrugged.

"All right," she said. "As long as the film is about me."

The light turns red and I look at Flint's camera to make sure it's still working. I duct-taped it to a light post across the street. I stood on a garbage bin to put it as high as I could. Flint wants the film to look as if it has been taken by a security camera. It's recording. I hope it works all right in the nighttime. But there's no way I would do what we're about to do in the day.

Holiday puts the car I rented in gear and pulls out of the parking spot down the street. She's wearing the dress Flint gave me. It's an evening dress, the sort of thing you'd wear to the theatre if people still went to the theatre. She drives up to the intersection. I work on keeping my breath steady. I try to keep my hands from trembling. When she stops at the line, I step out of the doorway of the furniture store and jump onto the hood of the car. I don't worry about dents. I rented the car with the credit card and driver's licence of another victim. I wave the gun at Holiday. She screams and goes to lock the door. I jump off the hood and open the door before she can.

"I want it all," I say. This is Holiday's script. But what she does next isn't in the script.

She pulls a canister out of her purse and waves it in my direction. Pepper spray. She doesn't pull the trigger, but I still almost lose the gun trying to get out of the way. She tosses the canister onto the passenger seat and tries to close the door. She slams it on my arm and I almost drop the gun again as the car rolls forward. She's playing this for real.

I rip open the door and hit her across the face with the gun before I even realize I'm doing it. Blood splatters on the windshield and she falls back into the passenger seat.

I try to think of something to say to apologize, but she only smiles at me and laughs.

I pull myself into the driver's seat and hit the brakes halfway through the intersection. I close the door and turn to see if she's all right.

"What were you doing?" I ask.

"Improv," she says.

I can't stop myself from putting my free hand on her cheek to feel the warmth of her blood.

That's when the cops arrive.

The police car rolls through the intersection. At first I think it's Flint making a surprise appearance. I wonder how he's found us. I think maybe there's some sort of GPS device in the dress, or maybe the gun. Then I see there are two cops in the car, and neither one is Flint.

They stare at Holiday and me, at the blood on the windshield, and I drop my hand from Holiday and look up at the traffic light, pretending not to see them.

"Did you call these guys?" Holiday asks. "Because I would have come up with a different script if I'd known we had extras."

Then I remember the mask I'm wearing and the gun in my hand. The cops turn on their lights and siren. They get out of their car and run behind it, yelling into their shoulder mikes.

For a second I think about trying to explain the situation. I think I could ask them if they know Flint. Then I see their guns and drop my own and step on the gas and go through the intersection. Holiday leans out the window.

"Help me!" she screams at the cops.

"What are you doing?" I ask her.

"Staying in character," she says. She smears the blood on her face to make it look worse.

I turn at the next intersection. The mask shifts on my face as I look behind us for the cops, and I can't see for several seconds.

THE WARHOL GANG 133

We side-swipe a row of parked cars, and Holiday and I are thrown into each other. Alarms go off behind us. The car spins in a full circle before I regain control. Holiday screams into the night.

The cops catch up to us after a few blocks. I watch them in the rear-view mirror.

"They're probably going to shoot out our tires or ram us," I say. That's what they do in the videos on *Panoptical.*

I imagine the footage, taken from the dashboard cameras. The police car crashing into the back of the rented car, spotlights trained on me inside.

"If you stop and let me go, I promise I'll put in a good word for you," Holiday says.

I imagine the car jammed against the side of a building, the cops dragging me from it, beating me with their clubs, kicking me like Flint did.

The car starts to slow. I realize I've taken my foot off the gas.

"Maybe we should just give up," I say. "We haven't done anything wrong. Have we?"

"I don't know about that," Holiday says, shaking her head, "but we certainly haven't done anything right."

In the rear-view mirror, I see another police car farther back, racing to catch up.

Then I see spotlights sweeping the sky beside me, and a parking lot. The mall. I hit the brakes and turn into the lot.

"Now what are you doing?" Holiday asks.

"We can hide here," I say.

But I realize as soon as I see the lot that I've made a mistake. All the cars in it are wrecked. I've turned in to a junkyard.

I stop and look behind us, but it's too late. The cops are there, blocking the way out.

"I'll tell them you treated me well," Holiday says. "That should count for something."

A man steps out of a trailer office at the entrance and stares at us and the cops. He holds up his hand. I don't have any other choice. I hit the gas pedal again and speed into the lot.

I take us down a row of scorched tanker trucks, then down a row of crushed school buses.

"I don't think there's any way out of this," Holiday says. "We should probably call it a wrap. Before something goes wrong." For some reason she laughs at that.

I turn again at an intersection of crumpled taxis and a pyramid of motorcycles. I wonder if Anthony's motorcycle is in there somewhere. I keep driving deeper into the junkyard, turning every chance I get, until I can't see the cops behind us anymore, and I don't know where we are.

"You can let me out anywhere," Holiday says.

Then things get strange. We turn left at the end of a row of ruined BMWs—burned, crushed, roofless, split in half—only to find a white wall in front of us. We hit the wall before I can find the brakes. But it's not a real wall—it's a plastic sheet. We rip through it and emerge into a parking lot of new BMWs. They gleam under lights on tall posts, like the kind you see on football fields. They're so new they have stickers on their windshields, and some of them even have plastic wrap on their hoods.

We're in a dealership—I can see the main building at the centre of the lot, under more lights.

I look back to see the cops follow us through the hole in the wall. On this side the plastic is covered with an image of a road beside the ocean. The police cruisers drive out of the sky. They're going slower now. I think they probably don't want to damage any of the cars on this lot.

We drive past the dealership building, and salesmen and customers inside watch us pass, then turn to watch the cops with their flashing lights and sirens. Holiday undoes her seat belt and gets ready to open the door to jump out, but I don't stop or even slow down. Then she points through the windshield. "The mall!" she says.

And it is. For real this time. Across the street from the dealership. Stores with more lights. Another Gap. A Sears. A Cineplex. A mall entrance. We drive toward it.

I'm so distracted by the lights I don't even see the barricade. One of those spike things on the ground to prevent people from driving cars off the lot. It smashes our tires, and the steering wheel is ripped from my hands. The car fishtails across the street. By the time I get my hands back on the wheel, it's too late.

Holiday screams as we drive up onto the sidewalk. People with shopping bags jump away from us on either side, holding the bags up like shields. We hit the doors leading into the mall. I close my eyes and wait to be impaled by something. Metal on metal. I'm thrown around the inside of the car. Gunshots. When I open my eyes again, my face is stinging like I've been punched. The inside of the car is filled with smoke. The car's blown airbags are in our laps.

We're driving down the inside of the mall, the car lurching

and thumping on its ruined tires. More smoke from beneath the hood.

Holiday keeps screaming, but when I look over at her I see it's a laughing scream. She claps her hands together.

The car's going slowly enough that I can steer around more people with bags. But when I try to stop, nothing happens. There's something wrong with the brakes. I look in the rearview. The cops have halted in the shattered entrance to the mall. They get out of their cars, guns in hand, and watch us drive away.

We turn a corner and go past a food court. People pause in eating their meals to stare at us. Every now and then someone thumps against the side of the car, but when I look in the rearview they're getting up and running away. No true victims.

"There," Holiday says and points to a hallway marked with washroom signs. The car is moving slowly enough now that we're able to open the doors and jump out. I turn to watch the car roll away, deeper into the mall. People film it with their phones. Then Holiday grabs me and pulls me down the hallway, past the washrooms and through an unmarked door in the wall.

Now we're in a tunnel lined with the back doors of stores. Holiday turns to me and takes off my Warhol mask. I'd forgotten I was still wearing it.

"Where have you been all my life?" she asks. She kisses me. Her face is sticky from her blood. I'm so surprised I don't even kiss her back.

Then she leads me down the tunnel to an empty loading dock. A rusted door on the far side opens up into another hallway, this one with burned-out lights. We walk in the darkness, me hanging on to her. Things crunch underneath my feet. I don't want to know what.

"Where are you taking me?" I ask.

"To the base," she says.

The base is an abandoned street in the foundations of the mall.
The mall has built around it, so it's cut off, surrounded by concrete walls on all sides. The only entrance I can see is the door
we come through. Pillars rise from the broken pavement of the
street to support girders and more concrete overhead. Lights
and cables hang from the girders. The street is lined with old
stores. Centretown Drugstore. Lee's Dry Cleaning. The Hollywood Cinema. Earl's Gas. I don't recognize any of these chains.
I don't even see a Starbucks.

"Where are we?" I ask.

"We're in the mall," Holiday says.

"This isn't the mall," I say. I stop when I see other people. A
man and woman sitting in lawn chairs in the front window of the
dry cleaner's. A naked man working out with free weights inside
the Blue Skies Travel Agency. A group of street kids sitting on
yoga mats in the gas station's parking lot, sorting through piles
of clothes. I see the man with the barcode tattoo from the Gap,
putting shirts in the empty bags he stole.

"It's all the mall," another man says, coming out of a building
that looks like a bank. The sign above the front doors has been
removed, leaving behind only holes in the wall. Someone has
spray-painted the word Resist! where the sign was. He reaches
out to Holiday's face and examines her wound. I realize I've seen

him before. He's the man with the scar who sold me the scanner in the spy-gear store. The other people in the base pause what they're doing to watch him.

"I know you," I tell him.

He looks at me, at Holiday's blood on my face.

"This is Che," Holiday says to me. "Che, this is . . ." She pauses and then says, "I don't know your name."

"Trotsky," I say.

Che smiles at that.

"You showed me the scanner," I say to him.

Che studies me for a few seconds, then nods. "And it changed your life, right?" He has the kind of voice that vibrates through you and makes you feel warm inside. Like the evangelist I saw on the screen in the cinema.

I nod. He's right. It did change my life. I wonder how he knows.

"And now you're here to join the resistance," he says.

"What resistance?" I ask.

"Trotsky's his own resistance," Holiday tells Che, laughing. "We just came back from a mission."

Che looks at her. "I didn't have you scheduled for another mission," he says. He looks back at me. "What have you done?"

"You'll see it on the news," Holiday says and leads me into the Hollywood Cinema. Che watches us go but doesn't say anything.

The Hollywood Cinema is small inside, with an old screen and seats for only a few hundred people. Someone's dressing room has been set up on the stage. A makeup table with a mirror and lights and boxes of makeup scattered on its surface.

Wigs hanging from a coat rack. Rolling racks of clothes. It's also someone's bedroom up there. A wardrobe and chairs. An Ikea bed. Padded handcuffs hanging from the bedposts.

"What is all this?" I ask.

"This is where I live," Holiday says.

We climb a stepladder onto the stage. Holiday sits at a table with a laptop and turns it on. I look at the mirror. There are photographs of people tucked into the frame. I don't recognize any of them, so Holiday names them off for me.

Jayne Mansfield.

Natalie Wood.

James Dean.

There's also the same photo we saw in the furniture store, the woman lying dead on the roof of the car. I touch her body without thinking about it.

"Beautiful, isn't she?" Holiday says.

"Who is she?" I ask.

"Evelyn McHale," Holiday says. "Jumped off the Empire State Building when her relationship ended. She could have just been another anonymous housewife, but she made herself famous."

The movie screen suddenly glows with light and I stumble backwards, nearly falling off the stage. It's not a film—it's the screen from Holiday's computer projected up there. I look at the icons looming over me. Holiday opens a web browser and starts scanning news sites.

"What are you looking for?" I ask.

But then I see exactly what she's looking for when she stops on *Panoptical*. Paris shows us a video of three men with guns robbing another man in a mall washroom somewhere. None of their guns are as nice as Flint's. Paris shows us two cars smashing into each other and bursting into flames at an intersection with failed traffic lights. Paris shows us a car driving down the inside of the mall, people scrambling to get out of its way.

"That's us," I say.

"*That's* us," Holiday says, nodding at the screen.

I watch us jump out of the car. I'm still wearing the Warhol mask in the video, so I can't actually see myself. But Holiday's not wearing a mask. She looks up, directly into the security camera. Then the camera moves to follow the car down the mall and we disappear from sight.

"That's one of my best movies yet," Holiday says. She hits replay and opens an application to record the video.

"Are you an actor?" I ask.

"Everyone's an actor," she says, not looking away from the screen. "I'm a star."

"A star?" I ask.

"I've been in more movies than most people in Hollywood," she says.

I look at her again. I don't recognize her.

She shakes her head at me and opens another window, plays some more *Panoptical* videos.

I watch a woman in water wings at the beach. Holiday. The artificial shark swims over her and forces her under. Blood in the water.

I watch Holiday standing at the auto show in her wings. She

smiles at the men filming her with their phones. Someone in the crowd tosses something at her feet and there's an explosion. She's on fire. The men film her some more.

I watch a car crash through the doors of a Gap. I watch the firefighters drag Holiday out. I watch as I step into the frame and drape a jacket around her shoulders. I stare at myself on the big screen until she closes that window.

All the videos are taken from a distance. They're all silent. Security cameras.

I look at Holiday. She's been there in my life all along. I don't know what to say. The only thing I can manage is, "You're the star of security videos?"

"I'm the Marilyn Monroe of security videos," she says.

I have to get Flint's camera, so I leave her at the cinema. I tell her I'll call her. She laughs like she doesn't believe me, then looks back at her computer. I go out into the base again and find it deserted now. Everyone else is gone. I can't remember exactly how we got here, so I try to retrace my steps. I go down the street until I see a door in the wall. I go through it and down a hallway.

But the door at the end opens onto another base, not the mall. At least I think it's another base. It's another street of old stores. Only these stores are all empty. There's no sign of people anywhere, and the only light is a flickering glow at the end of the street. An escalator. It rises up into the mall, coming out in a partially constructed hallway. Exposed pipes and wiring on the walls. Lines drawn on the untiled floor where stores are supposed to be. A stack of metal beams with some empty coffee cups on them. Dust so thick I leave footprints.

I turn around to go back down again, but there is no down escalator.

I find my way home and take my car back to the intersection where we left the camera. But the camera is gone now. I look for it on the ground underneath the light post I taped it to, along the sidewalk, even in the garbage bins, but I can't find it. It's only then I realize I don't have the gun anymore either. It must still be in the rented car that drove off into the mall. I wonder what Flint will be more upset about: the loss of the camera or the loss of the gun.

By the time I'm done searching, the sky has turned grey. Dawn. I've been up the entire night. I go to work without going back home. I try to sleep in the pod, but I keep imagining the police coming for me.

I imagine cops riding the elevator up to the office, in full body armour, with the same assault rifles Reagan used at Gun World.

I imagine the cops opening the pod door and sticking their guns inside it.

I imagine the cops pulling the triggers.

I imagine feeling the bullets hit where Flint shot me.

Nickel congratulates me when he lets me out at the end of the day. "You're doing much better," he says.

I'm afraid to go home in case the cops are waiting for me there. I walk through the mall as slowly as I can. I look at the security cameras I can see, but I can't tell if they're watching me or not.

I stop in front of a Sony store when I see Paris on a monitor in the window. A Breaking News logo floats over her head like a halo. She's on all the monitors in the window. She's on all the monitors inside the store. Her voice comes from the store's speakers.

She tells me about an abduction.

She tells me about a shootout.

She tells me about a dangerous fugitive on the loose.

It takes me a moment to realize she's talking about me.

She shows me a video. I watch as I strike Holiday in the face with Flint's gun and climb into the rented car.

Then Paris shows me another clip, this one of the police chase. It's a montage taken from cameras in the police cruisers. The rented car bounces off parked cars, leaving a shower of sparks behind it. The soundtrack is sirens and scanner calls. It's just like I imagined it.

Paris interviews two cops involved in the pursuit. One wears a bandage around his head, while the other has his arm in a sling. The background behind them is the paused image of the rented car turning in to the junkyard. I can see the silhouette of my head through the back window.

"He was a real professional," the cop with the sling says. "Maybe ex-military."

"I felt a bullet go right past my head," the cop with the bandage says.

"What do you think he wants with the woman?" Paris asks.

"It was a carjacking, but he left the car," the cop with the sling says, shaking his head.

"We think maybe he's part of a gang," the cop with the bandage says.

"But what about the woman?" Paris asks.

Both cops shrug. "We really don't know," the one with the sling says. "Maybe it's a ransom-type thing."

"Or maybe he's a serial killer," the cop with the bandage says. "Or both." The two cops nod.

"Don't worry," the cop with the sling says. "We'll find her, dead or alive."

The paused video plays again, and for a few seconds I can see myself and Holiday side by side. When we turn our heads back to look at the cops, our silhouettes look like we're kissing.

"Remember," Paris says, "it could happen to you."

I lay my hand on the window separating me from the monitor. From Paris. From Holiday. From myself.

I call in sick to work the next day. I want to search for more footage of myself online. Flint phones while I'm eating breakfast and scanning the news sites.

"A shootout with police," Flint says.

"My wife still alive," Flint says.

"That wasn't the film I had in mind," Flint says.

"That wasn't the film we wanted to make," I say.

"Who was that actor?" Flint asks.

"She's nobody," I say.

"A nobody?" Flint asks.

"I found her at an accident," I say.

"So she's a Jane Doe," Flint says.

"Are you going to arrest me?" I ask.

"I'll be in touch," Flint says.

"We could do another film," I say.

"I've got a different film in mind now," Flint says. "A better film."

I call Holiday to talk to her about what Flint said.

"Never mind that," she says. "Have you seen the news?"

I wonder if she's going to turn me in to the police. There must be a reward for my arrest. I wonder where I can hide. For some reason I think about the house from HomeBrand.

"That was my biggest role yet, thanks to you," she says.

She tells me to meet her at a Club Monaco in the mall. She tells me to come in character. She disconnects before I can ask what that means.

I go to the Club Monaco. It's one of those multi-level stores, with a second floor overlooking the main level. I see Che browsing a wall of jeans. He's wearing a suit and tie today. I walk toward him but he shakes his head without so much as glancing at me.

My cellphone rings and I answer it. "Above you," Holiday says, and I look up to see her standing by the railing on the second floor. She's dyed her hair black, but I recognize her because of the dress she's wearing. Flint's dress.

I take the escalator up and join her by the railing.

"What are you doing?" I say, looking at the dress. "What if someone recognizes you?"

"That's the whole idea," she says. She takes a handful of scarves from a nearby table and holds them up. "I was thinking of adding my own touch, though. Which one of these do you like?"

I check the ceiling for security cameras. They're everywhere. And those are just the ones I can see.

"I don't want to go to jail," I say. "Or worse." I think I should leave, but I can't. I think about cops on their way here at this very moment, and I feel a rush, a little trace of what I experienced with Flint out in that field.

Holiday wraps one of the scarves around my neck and pulls me closer to her. We lean against the railing.

"I knew you'd come," she says. "Do you know how I knew that?"

She keeps leaning back, pulling me with her, until I have to grab hold of the railing on either side of her to keep my balance.

"Because you're like me," she says.

"I don't know what you mean," I say.

"I saw it in the mall," she says. "When you tried to kill us with the car."

"That was an accident," I say.

"Yes," she says and pulls me into a kiss. Her lips spark mine. Static electricity. She leans back even farther and I follow her. And then I realize the railing isn't stopping us anymore.

Holiday screams and I hear myself screaming for a second and we hang on to each other as we fall. We hit a display table piled with sweaters on the ground floor, and all the breath goes out of me. I lie there in the remains of the table with Holiday, trying to breathe again, but I can't. I open my mouth but my muscles won't work. My whole body is tingling, like when one of your limbs falls asleep. I look around for help. Holiday is beside me, her mouth opening and closing, too. I see that her hand is in mine, but I can't feel it.

People gather around us, some carrying Club Monaco bags, others wearing Club Monaco name tags. I think maybe they're going to help us, but they just stand and stare. Then my breath comes back, only it comes from inside of me. I roll to my side and throw up in the sweaters. I can suddenly hear again. I hadn't realized I couldn't until now. Alarms and more screams. I look up to see Che and others running out of the store with armfuls of jeans.

The pins-and-needles feeling turns into knives and hammers. I collapse back into the sweaters. I look back up at the railing. Part of it hangs loose and I know what's happened. Someone has removed the bolts holding it in place. And I know we didn't fall onto a table of sweaters by chance. I laugh, even though it makes me hurt more.

"It's all right," someone in the crowd tells me. "You're going to be all right."

"I know," I say.

Holiday's on her hands and knees now, trying to get up. She falls back into the sweaters, but I catch her in my arms. She looks at me and smiles.

"You're the first one who never let go," she whispers to me.

Then she looks over my shoulder for the security cameras.

We go to an emergency clinic in the mall. The paramedics the Club Monaco manager called drive us there in an emergency cart. It's like those luggage vehicles you see at airports, only there are stretchers attached to the back.

I'm feeling all right, just some lumps on my head and bruises on my torso, but Holiday says we need a medical record of our injuries.

"For the lawsuit," she says.

"What lawsuit?"

"Against the store," she says. "For the loose railing."

I shake my head. "They'll fight that," I say. "They'll figure out what happened."

"They'll settle," Holiday says. "It's cheaper than fighting it in court. It comes down to the money."

"They always settle," the paramedic who's driving says. The paramedic in the passenger seat asks us if we need anything for the pain. He shows us a case full of pills.

"I'm fine," I say.

The truth is, I'm feeling better than all right. I don't feel any pain at all. I feel like I've already taken some pills. I sit back and watch the stores pass. Their lights are brighter than I've ever seen them, the products inside more colourful and vibrant than anything I've ever owned. Their entrances have never looked so inviting.

It's just like what happened with Flint.

I don't feel anything but the memory of my kiss with Holiday. I want to do it again. I reach for her but she laughs and pushes me away.

"Not here," she says. "Save it for the cameras."

"You guys were lucky," the paramedic who offered us the pills says. "You should see some of the falling victims I've worked on."

I've never felt so alive.

The clinic could be the same one I went to after the man slashed me in the cinema. I'm not sure. It looks the same, but the nurses and doctors are different.

After one of the doctors checks us out and releases us with a warning to stay clear of Club Monacos, we go back to the base. It's decorated for a party now. Streamers hang from the buildings. Balloons are tied to the lampposts. Some folding tables have been set up in the middle of the street. One of them holds piles of clothes. The other holds cans of Coke and Pepsi and a cake.

Che and a couple of the others are there, sorting the clothes. The man with the barcode tattoo calls out sizes of jeans and Che enters the information on a laptop. A woman I saw at the gas station puts the jeans in shipping boxes as the man passes them to her. Che stops what he's doing when he sees us and applauds. The others look up and join in.

"What is this?" I ask.

"Welcome to the resistance," Che says. He tosses me a shirt and I look at it. It has a Club Monaco price tag. It's so new it almost seems to glow in my hands. The same sense of calm I usually get when I buy something mixes with the last remnants of the adrenalin high from my near-death experience with Holiday. Like a drug cocktail.

Che steps over to me and puts his hands on my shoulders, looks me in the eyes. "From now on you do your missions with us," he says. "From now on you'll never have to pay for anything again. Whatever you want, it's yours."

His words give me a whole new high. I think I don't even need pills anymore. I just need to spend more time with Holiday and Che and the rest of them. I feel so good I worry I'm imagining the whole scene. I worry I've imagined the Resist! slogans all along. I worry I've imagined Holiday.

The man with the tattoo waves me over to the table with the cake. There's writing on the icing. Happy Birthday, Richard.

"Who's Richard?" I ask.

Che reaches down and scoops the name away with a finger. He licks the icing from his finger and grins at me.

"That's you," he says. "You can be anybody you want to be now."

"Mao," the man with the barcode says, saluting.

"Patty Hearst," the woman says, performing a mock curtsy.

I realize then that everyone has a code name, like at Adsenses. I try to think of a code name, but I don't want to use Trotsky again. I say the only other name I can think of.

"Warhol."

They all smile and nod. Holiday cuts me a piece of cake.

"Welcome to the family," she says.

I hope that if I'm in the pod imagining all this, Nickel doesn't pull me out.

After we finish eating, Holiday and I go into the cinema. We sit in chairs in the audience while she checks *Panoptical*. Paris shows us a tanker truck on fire driving into a hotel somewhere, and people being blown out the windows. Paris shows us a burning hot-air balloon falling from the sky, the people inside it screaming. Paris shows us a house collapsed into a sinkhole, its residents waving for help from the windows as mud oozes in around them.

I can't stop thinking about what Holiday said to me. Family.

"What's your real name?" I ask her. I think real names are the sort of thing family members would know.

She looks at me. "What do you mean?"

"What's the name you grew up with?" I ask.

"Holiday," she says.

"That's not a code name?" I ask.

"It's my real name," she says, watching Paris show us a car hit by a train at a railway crossing. "My mother named me after the place of conception."

"She was on holiday?" I ask.

"A Holiday Inn," Holiday says.

"Which one?" I ask. I think maybe I can take her there. Surprise her with a getaway.

"She said there was only one," Holiday says. "She said the same thing about my father."

"What does your mother think about what you do?" I ask.

"I don't even know if she's still alive," Holiday says.

Paris shows us in the Club Monaco, falling together.

"Sometimes I imagine I'm her when I play my roles," Holiday says.

She records the Club Monaco video. When she's done, she plays it back and watches it again.

"We could have died," I point out.

"That's what makes it a good role," she says. "That's what makes people remember you."

We crash into the table again and people rush to help us again. I don't know what she's talking about.

"What about Social?" I say. "What kind of role is that?"

She shrugs. "I only work at Social when I need the money. That's more about auditions than roles for me."

"Auditions for what?" I ask.

"Private films," she says.

"What kind of private films?" I ask.

"Home movies," she says.

I fall asleep in the chair watching *Panoptical,* but pain wakes me later. I'm sore all over. Holiday and I are gone now, the screen blank. I get up, but I can barely stand. Every part of my body seems to be throbbing at different times. I think I need some more adrenalin. I wonder if they sell adrenalin at PharmaWorld.

Holiday is asleep in her bed, but I'm too stiff to climb on to the stage. I hear people talking in the street so go out into the base instead. I think maybe more clothes from the Club Monaco may make me feel better.

It's Che and a FedEx courier by the tables. The courier is pushing a trolley of shipping boxes. The same shipping boxes Patty Hearst and Mao were filling earlier. I don't see any of the clothes from the Club Monaco now. The courier hands Che an invoice and heads down the street with the trolley. Che watches him go with a smile on his face.

"Are those the clothes you guys took?" I ask Che, and he nods.

"We have regular buyers for most of our merchandise," he says.

We watch the courier disappear. I feel that hollowness inside again.

"So the resistance is just a bunch of thieves?" I ask.

Che looks at me. The smile on his face is like Nickel's smile now: it doesn't reach his eyes. "I'm not a thief," he says, the warmth gone from his voice. "Are you a thief?"

I look down at the Club Monaco shirt I'm wearing over my other one. The price tag is still attached. I don't know how to answer his question.

"We take what we need to survive," Che says. "To liberate ourselves. But we still have bills to pay. We have to buy off mall staff to pretend not to know about the base. We have to pay off workers in stores so we can do our missions. We have to pay couriers to make special trips down here." He shakes his head. "We're a revolution, but we're not a non-profit."

"So what exactly does the resistance resist?" I ask.

Che picks up the last piece of cake from the table and starts eating it out of his hand.

"Everything we can," he says.

I go past Thatcher and the car on the way to work. Thatcher is rolling around on the hood with the man who talked to me the last time I stopped here. They're clawing at each other's faces, elbowing each other. The other man and the woman sit on the trunk and watch. The crowd around the car is standing room only. People cheer the fight and film the scene with their phones. The car is covered in bloodstains now.

I push my way through the crowd and try to go to Thatcher's side, but the car is blocked off by caution tape and security guards. One of the guards pushes me back when I duck under the tape.

"This is for authorized personnel only," he says. "And I know that's not you."

"But they're fighting," I point out.

The guard nods. "The only rule is they have to maintain contact with the vehicle at all times," he says.

Thatcher gets the other man in a chokehold. The man claws at Thatcher's melted face, but Thatcher doesn't let go. He hangs on until the other man turns red and stops flailing his arms and kicking, then holds on a few seconds longer before shoving the man off the car. The security guards finally move, a couple of them running over and dragging the unconscious man away, into the crowd, which is cheering even louder now. Some people exchange money, others take more photos or videos.

Thatcher rolls over on the hood, gasping and weeping. He wraps his arms around the car's windshield. He gazes through the bloody glass.

"I am not here," he says.

I go back to the base after work. There are more people living in the stores now. A man irons shirts in the front window of the post office. A woman makes lattes with a gleaming espresso maker inside the Chinese Star restaurant. The front window is broken and she hands the lattes to two men in suits waiting outside. They take their lattes and go back in the direction of the mall. I've never seen any of these people before.

I go into the cinema and find Holiday putting on her makeup. She's wearing Flint's dress again. She's dyed her hair silver. The lights from the makeup table give her a halo.

"Who are all those other people?" I ask.

"New members," Holiday says without looking away from her reflection. "The word about us is getting out."

"How?" I ask.

"They all saw the movie where you kidnapped me," she says. "People talk. They tell their friends. Their friends find their way here."

I go to climb the stepladder but it's just a hallucination. I stumble and fall to the ground instead. "Jesus!" I say. I look around and see the real stepladder at the other end of the stage.

"I think I need a new mission," I say.

Holiday looks down at me. "Why else would you be here?" she says.

The mission involves one of the new members of the resistance. Che talks to us in the street outside and tells us the man's name is Sony. Che says he's named after the place he works. I'm glad I called myself Warhol rather than Adsenses.

Che says a Sony store is the target. Che says Sony is waiting for us. Che says he's undercover, so we won't know which Sony store employee he is. Che says it's classic guerrilla strategy. Che puts his hands on my shoulders and looks me in the eyes.

"The success of this mission is up to you," he says. "You're the most important person in the world right now." His words make me feel better than any of the visions I've had of myself in the pod. I forget all about him selling the clothes from the Club Monaco. I want to hug him and thank him, but I'm afraid I'll weep if I do.

This is the mission.

Holiday and I go to the Sony store in the mall. We're posing as newlyweds. Holiday says newlyweds are inherently dramatic, but I don't know anything about that. We wear rings I've taken from accident victims.

We ask one of the sales clerks to show us video cameras. His name tag just says Sony. All the clerks' name tags say Sony.

"It's for the honeymoon," Holiday tells him.

The sales clerk takes us to a wall of video cameras. I wonder

THE WARHOL GANG 163

if he's Sony or a regular sales clerk. He looks at me, and I know it's my turn to say something. I wish we had a script.

"Which one do you suggest?" I ask, and he lifts one of the cameras from the wall and hands it to me. I turn it on and film Holiday. She blows kisses into the camera and laughs. It's like she really is my wife. I don't want to let go of the camera.

"Can we see it on a monitor?" she asks.

The clerk takes us into a display room full of wide-screen monitors attached to the walls. He plugs the camera into one of the monitors and hands it to me. The power's off, so I turn it back on.

There's an explosion, and then I'm on the floor, convulsing and trying to scream as I burn, but I can't breathe. Holiday convulses beside me. Then it fades as the sales clerk kicks the camera from my hand. There wasn't an explosion after all. I'm not really on fire. It takes me a few seconds to understand.

A short circuit.

We were electrocuted.

I still can't breathe.

Sony yells for help, and then the edges of my vision fade away. All I can see are the monitors floating in the darkness above me. They're all playing the feed from the camera. Holiday and me, lying dead on the floor. I see her hand in mine. I don't remember her grabbing hold. She must have done it when she saw me getting shocked.

I drift up toward the monitors. Toward Holiday and me. I feel warmth spreading through my body. I think this is what it must be like to be born again.

Then I fall back to the floor and all the pain comes back and I finally manage to breathe again and scream. I look down and see the warmth is from pissing myself. I look over at Holiday. She's gasping for breath as well, but her hand is still in mine.

The alarms go off at the front of the store, and more people start screaming.

After different paramedics take us to a different clinic and different doctors tell us we'll be all right as long as we avoid electrical appliances, I ask Holiday if she wants to go on a date. We're standing outside the clinic, looking at the mannequins in the window of a Gap store. They're being changed for a new display, so they're all naked. I'm feeling the same high as before, like after the Club Monaco and after Flint. I can't stop thinking about Holiday holding my hand. I think maybe I've finally found someone. Like in the photos of all those accident victims. Only this time it's really my life.

"I thought we *were* dating," Holiday says and laughs.

We go to Metro, an amusement park in the mall. We ride a roller coaster that keeps going off its rails. I think we're going to die the first time, but then I realize it's part of the ride. I put my hands in the air and scream along with Holiday.

We wander through a hall of mirrors and get separated. Everywhere I look, all I see is myself.

We go to the You're History Experience, where each room has a different hologram history show.

We stand in a hologram crowd on a street and watch Kennedy get shot as he drives past.

We stand in a hologram crowd in a parking lot and watch the space shuttle blow up over our heads.

We stand in a hologram crowd on a beach and watch a tsunami wash over us.

Other people stand in the crowds with us and cheer the disasters. When the scenes end, the holograms fade away for a few seconds, leaving the rooms empty except for the real people. Then the holograms start at the beginning again. The park is open twenty-four hours. Hologram messages between the scenes say the loops never stop.

We stand in a crowd that watches the World Trade Center towers come down. We reach for each other and kiss as the cloud of ash and office papers and coffee cups and other debris engulfs us.

Then the hologram fades and it's just the two of us, alone in the empty room.

Then Flint calls.

"I'm ready for my new film," Flint says.

"We can still do the film you wanted," I tell him.

"I want another film now," Flint says.

"And bring my wife," Flint says.

I pick up Holiday and we drive to the address Flint gives us. Holiday wears Flint's wife's dress. I try to imagine what she's thinking but I can't. I wonder what Flint's thinking but I can't imagine that either. I'm so distracted I run a red light.

"This is not the time for that," Holiday says. "I don't want to be a real accident victim."

The address is a tower just like my apartment building. Elevators lead to the floors above and the mall below. We take one to the condo where Flint waits. Holiday looks at her reflection in the elevator mirror. I ask her what she's thinking.

"I'm thinking about my character," she says.

"What character?" I ask.

"Me," she says.

When Flint opens the door to the condo, he's wearing his uniform and bulletproof vest. The camera he'd given me to use the night of the police chase is set up on a stand in a corner of the room. Pieces of duct tape still hang from it.

"You can't imagine what I had to do to get that from the evidence room," Flint tells me. He looks at Holiday. "I didn't think you'd still have the dress," he says.

"Wardrobe is your co-star," Holiday says.

"If you say so," Flint says and closes and locks the door behind us.

I look around. The layout of the place is almost the same as my place. The furniture is variations of my furniture. The only real difference is the view of the condo tower across the street.

Flint goes over to a bar in the corner and pours himself a Scotch. When he comes back, he pulls a Warhol mask from one of his pockets and tosses it to me.

"You're fugitives," he says. "Do you know what that means?"

I don't say anything. I look down at the mask in my hands. It stares back at me.

"It means I can do anything I want," Flint says.

"Sounds like I'm going to need a drink myself," Holiday says.

Flint smiles at her. "If I'd met you instead of marrying her, maybe I wouldn't have to do this," he says.

"I doubt it," Holiday says.

"Wait here," Flint tells her and leads me to the bedroom.

Holiday sits on the couch and looks around. "This is pretty much the way I pictured it," she says.

The bedroom looks like any of the bedrooms in the places I break in to: a bed, a couple of wardrobes, some photos on the walls. The only difference is this place has a telescope by the window. It's dark in here, but there's enough light from the other room to see Flint taking out his gun.

My mouth goes dry and my legs almost give out underneath me. I'm suddenly aware of my heart pounding in my chest, and then adrenalin flushes through me once more. I think Flint's going to shoot me again, and this time I'm not wearing the bulletproof vest. But instead he hands me the gun.

"I want to know what it feels like," he tells me.

I forget how heavy the gun is and almost drop it when I take it. I look at it, then back at him.

"What do you mean?" I ask.

"Just remember, aim for the vest," he says. He goes into the other room, leaving me there standing in the dark.

I watch them through the doorway. Flint pours Holiday a drink and sits beside her on the couch. He puts his hand on her knee. "Your name is Monaco," he says.

Holiday sips from her drink and shakes her head. "No, it's not," she says. "It's Holiday."

Flint runs his hand down the side of her face, then grabs her by the throat. "You can be whoever you want with him," he says. "But tonight, with me, you're my wife. Your name is Monaco."

I don't want to see this. I go over to the window and look at the condos across the street. I watch a man and woman make dinner in their kitchen. I watch a man talk on the phone in his bedroom. I watch a woman watch a show on a monitor I can't see in her living room. Some of the other condos have telescopes in their windows, too. Others have cameras on stands. I put on the Warhol mask. I don't want to be recognized if someone is looking at me.

But I can't help myself from going back to watch Flint and Holiday.

Flint goes over to the camera and hits the record button. When he comes back, he slaps Holiday across the face. She looks up at him and takes another sip of her drink.

"Why don't you hit me like you'd really hit your wife," she says.

Flint slaps her again, harder this time. Her cheek turns red from the blow.

I look at the photos on the walls of the bedroom. They show a man and woman in different places around the world: on a tropical beach, riding an elephant, leaning against the railing of a cruise ship, skydiving together. The man in the photos isn't Flint. I wonder if the woman is Flint's wife. I wonder if Flint has broken in to this place.

I look back out into the other room. I watch Flint climb onto Holiday and kiss her. I watch Holiday thrust up against him and bite his lips. I watch Flint hit her in the face with an elbow, knocking her back. I watch Holiday wrap her legs around him and pull him closer, smash him in the face with her forehead. I watch Flint wrap his hands around her neck and choke her. I watch Holiday look at me.

It's the same look she gave me at the auto show, when the wings were melted into her skin. When she wanted someone to save her.

I go into the other room and try to pull Flint off her. "That's enough," I say. "You're hurting her. For real."

Flint doesn't let go of her. He doesn't glance my way.

"You'll have to kill me," he says.

I grab Flint in an embrace and try to pull him off Holiday, who's thrashing now as she struggles to breathe, but it's like I'm not even there. I can't move him. I try to imagine what he would do in my place.

I try to shoot him in the back with the gun but the trigger doesn't move. The safety. I look at the gun, but I don't know how to even find the safety. Holiday makes whining noises and her eyes bulge at me.

I drop the gun to the floor and run into the bedroom and grab the telescope. I go back into the other room and smash it down on Flint's head. A spray of blood hits Holiday's face, the couch, my shoes. Flint collapses into Holiday's arms and doesn't move.

Holiday sits up and takes a deep breath, like someone who's just surfaced from underwater, then coughs and gags. She pushes Flint away and he falls off the couch to the floor, on his back. He stares up at the ceiling lights. He doesn't blink.

"I think you killed him," Holiday gasps.

I poke Flint with the telescope but he doesn't move at all. I lean on the telescope and try to catch my own breath. Try to stop my shaking.

"I didn't mean to," I say.

Holiday looks up at me. "Are you sure?" she asks.

"It was an accident," I say.

I kneel beside Flint and lay my hand on his neck. I can feel his sweat, his skin, but I can't feel his pulse. I touch my lips to his but can't feel his breath. I look into his eyes and wonder if he sees me.

I don't want to take my hands off him.

I've never felt this close to anyone.

Holiday gets up and staggers to the bathroom. She throws up in the sink and then looks at herself in the mirror.

I take off Flint's uniform, just like he took it off me in the field. His bulletproof vest, his holster. His badge and shirt. I stop every few seconds to feel his neck again. No pulse. Nothing. I can feel his flesh cooling beneath my hand. At least I think I can.

"What are you doing?" Holiday asks me, adjusting her dress as she comes out of the bathroom.

"We need to take anything with us that has our DNA on it," I say. "That's how they catch people on the cop shows."

I don't tell her I want to take his uniform home with me and wear it again.

"I don't think they're going to have a problem figuring out who we are," Holiday says, looking out the window. I follow her gaze.

People in the building across the street watch us. They talk on phones. They film us with their cameras.

"We have to get out of here," I say.

Holiday watches the people watching us as I run into the kitchen and grab a garbage bag for Flint's gear. Then she nods to herself and reaches down to the floor to pick up Flint's gun.

"Stay in character," she tells me.

"What character?" I ask as I fill the bag.

"You're part of a gang," she says. "Remember?" She doesn't look away from the other building.

"What gang?" I say. "What are you talking about?" I consider putting the bloody telescope in the bag, too, but there's no room with the vest and boots and the rest of it.

"The cops said you were in a gang," she says. "In that movie where you abducted me. This is the sequel now."

"This isn't a movie," I tell her.

"Everything is a movie," she says.

"Besides, there isn't any gang," I point out as I tie the bag shut. I touch Flint one last time. He's definitely colder now. "There's just me," I say, heading for the door.

"No, not anymore," Holiday says. She looks down at the gun and flicks something on it with her hand. The safety I couldn't find. "Don't you remember the first thing you ever said to me?" she asks.

I look at her. I don't remember.

She raises the gun and fires several shots at the other building. The condo window shatters and the shards of glass fall out of sight. Windows break in the other building and people drop.

"You are not alone," Holiday says.

I have to lean against the wall of the elevator for support. I can't stop shaking. I don't know if it's from killing Flint or Holiday shooting at the other people.

"What the hell were you doing back there?" I ask.

"Every good movie needs a plot twist," Holiday says. She looks at her reflection in the elevator mirror and fixes her hair. "Now they're going to think I'm in the gang, too. They'll want to know more about me."

"But there is no gang," I point out again.

"You have to give the audience what they want," Holiday says.

We reach the lobby but don't go outside. We can't see the cops, but the windows flash red and blue from the lights of a police car somewhere. I think I could be in a sniper scope right now.

We go down into the mall instead. Holiday pulls the mask from my head and stuffs it into her purse along with the gun before the doors open. I'd forgotten I was still wearing the mask.

She takes out her phone and makes a call. "We're on our way," she says. "Get things ready." She listens for a few seconds and then smiles. "You won't believe it," she says. "I think we've just gone blockbuster."

"Who was that?" I ask when she disconnects, but she just shakes her head again.

"Right now you need to focus on your character," she says. "And at this particular moment your character is someone who disappears in a crowd."

We go out into the mall and walk past coffee shops and phone stores until we reach an intersection. Holiday leads me down the hallway with the most shoppers. I keep looking over my shoulder but I don't see any police. I've stopped shaking and now I don't feel anything at all. But I know I should feel something. I wonder if I'm getting sick again. I hold the bag with Flint's gear closer to my chest.

Holiday takes us to a PharmaWorld. We go up and down the aisles until we find Che in the home appliances section, pushing a cart piled with boxes from the shelves. Coffee makers, cutlery sets, toaster ovens. He's wearing a PharmaWorld shirt. He hands us two more PharmaWorld shirts from his cart.

"Just throw them on over what you're wearing," he says. "Hopefully you won't need to pass any close inspection."

"What does that mean, 'hopefully'?" I ask. "What are you doing here?" I look at Holiday. "What are *we* doing here?"

They don't answer me. Instead, Che takes us down the aisle and nods at a man and woman we pass. They nod back. I've never seen them before. I turn to watch them and see the man stick his left hand in a blender on a shelf. He takes a deep breath and says something to the woman. She sticks the cord of the blender into her purse. The blender turns on and the man screams as the inside turns red.

I can't believe what I'm seeing and try to stop, but Che picks up his pace, heading for the rear of the store, and Holiday drags me along after him. I want to go back to the man, who's fallen to the floor, screaming and clutching at his mangled hand. I think I must be imagining this. I want to see if he's really real. But Holiday won't let go of me.

"That's us," I tell her.

Holiday shakes her head. "Not anymore," she says. "We're bigger than that now."

Some more people in PharmaWorld shirts come out a back door and run past us, toward the screaming. Che stops the door from closing with his cart, and we go into the stockroom. It's row after row of boxes on shelves. It reminds me of the auto junkyard.

Che leads us up and down the aisles like he knows where he's going, but I'm soon lost. At one point, we pass two men in PharmaWorld shirts going in the opposite direction. They nod at us and we nod back. I have no idea if they work for the store or they're more members of the resistance.

Che opens another door and we go out into a mall staff tunnel. Che pulls off his PharmaWorld shirt. He's wearing a Che T-shirt underneath. He takes a can of spray paint from somewhere in the cart and paints Resist! on the PharmaWorld door.

I throw up. It happens so quickly I don't even have time to bend down, and I get it all over the front of my shirt.

Che looks back and forth between Holiday and me. "What happened?" he asks.

"We killed the cop," Holiday says.

Che studies me. "Really," he says.

"It was real, all right," Holiday says. She shakes her head like she doesn't believe it. "We're celebrities now," she says.

I throw up again, but this time nothing comes out. I gasp for air. I look up and down the tunnel. It stretches out of sight in either direction, lined with the back doors of stores. I don't know where I am.

Che puts the spray paint back in his bag. He puts his hands on my shoulders. He holds me up when I want to fall.

"I said you were important, didn't I?" he tells me.

"*We're* important," Holiday says and he nods at her.

"Of course," he says. "But you weren't killing cops before Warhol came along, were you?"

I feel the heat of Che's hands on my skin. I want to confess to him. I want to tell him I didn't mean to kill Flint. But then he kisses me and hugs me, despite the vomit and blood on my shirt.

"I believed in you, and look at what you've become," he says, and I feel his faith in me. I know I did the right thing, even if I didn't mean to do it.

Then he releases me. "Now let's go back to the base and celebrate," he says.

But the base is already celebrating by the time we get there.

The street is crowded with people now, some I recognize from my other visits, some I don't. More bike couriers, more people in suits, more people who look like anyone else in the mall.

They cheer and applaud when we walk down the street. People reach out to touch me and Holiday. I feel like a fighter getting ready to enter the ring.

"Now that's resistance!" someone yells, and others call out their agreement.

I look at Che, but he just shrugs. "I haven't told anyone yet," he says while waving at the crowd. "I haven't had time."

"Someone must have posted a video," Holiday says.

The three of us go into the cinema and Holiday wakes her laptop from sleep. Her browser is already at *Panoptical,* so all she has to do is refresh it. The first video Paris shows us is Holiday struggling with Flint. It's taken from across the street, so there's no sound other than the breathing of the man holding the camera.

I watch Flint pin Holiday to the couch and strike her with his elbow.

I watch as I enter the frame wearing a Warhol mask and hit Flint with the telescope.

I watch Holiday shoot out the window, and the screen blurs as the cameraman drops to the floor for cover.

Paris shows us another video. It's the same scene taken from a different angle, a few floors up.

I watch Flint struggle with Holiday.

I watch as I enter the frame wearing a Warhol mask and hit Flint with the telescope.

"Come look at this," the woman filming the scene yells.

I watch Holiday shoot out the window. The woman screams and drops to the floor, the image blurring and then refocusing on the bottom of a couch.

"We're famous," Holiday breathes. She doesn't take her eyes off the screen.

Che doesn't say anything for a moment. Then he nods and smiles. He heads for the door. "I'll make sure the proper message about this gets out," he says.

Holiday keeps replaying the videos. I climb on the stage and sit on her bed. I look at myself in the makeup mirror. I strip down until I'm naked. I pull Flint's clothes from the bag and look at them. I feel the blood on them. It's dried already.

I wonder if I'm hallucinating this and I dry heave a little more.

Holiday sits beside me on the bed and holds me. She strokes my hair. I don't know what she's doing for a moment. Then I remember the video of the woman holding her dead son. I cling to her.

When I look up at her before I fall asleep, she's still watching the big screen.

When I wake, Holiday floats in the darkness above me. She points a gun at me. It takes me a moment to realize I'm not in the pod, that what I'm seeing is on the cinema screen.

I turn to find Holiday asleep in the bed beside me. She's still wearing the dress.

I look back at the screen. The image is better quality than the other videos I watched earlier. It's shot from a closer range. Inside the condo.

Flint's camera.

I get up and go over to the laptop. Hit the button to play the video from the start.

A black bar covers Holiday's crotch as she struggles with Flint on the couch. A caption at the bottom of the screen says Breaking News! Warhol Gang Kills Cop!

I wonder what the Warhol Gang is for a moment, and then I realize the caption means me. And Holiday.

"She's joined them now," Paris's voice says. "Police think it's a case of Stockholm Syndrome."

I don't know what Stockholm Syndrome is.

"It's when kidnapping victims fall in love with their captors," Paris says. "Like when that woman fell in love with those people who made her rob banks."

I watch as I step into the scene wearing the Warhol mask. I watch as I try to free Holiday from Flint but fail.

"Police are trying to determine why they broke into the condo," Paris says. "Maybe to steal things for the gang. Maybe to kidnap more people and make more gang members. Maybe we'll never know."

I watch as I try to shoot Flint but can't figure out the gun.

"Police tell us Officer Flint was off duty but was the first to respond," Paris says.

I watch as I strike Flint with the telescope. I watch as I lay my hands on him.

"He died a hero," Paris says.

Holiday picks up the gun and shoots out the window.

"You are not alone!" she says.

The image fades to Paris in her newsroom.

"Remember," she says, "it could happen to you."

When the video ends, I read the comments people have posted.

Good job, bro.

You guys are a great couple.

Hope to hook up with you on a mission.

All the comments have the same poster name: "Resist!"

There are hundreds of them. I'm skimming them when Holiday rolls over and tells me to come to bed. She tells me to put the Paris video on a loop. She tells me to put on Flint's uniform.

I do the things she tells me and get into bed with her. On the screen, Flint and Holiday struggle on the couch. Flint climbs onto Holiday and kisses her.

Holiday straddles me and kisses me. She bites my lips, drawing blood, as she undoes my pants. I already have an erection.

Flint hits Holiday with an elbow, knocking her back.

Holiday slips my cock out of my pants and slides down onto me. She's wet. She closes her eyes but doesn't make any sound.

Holiday wraps her legs around Flint and pulls him closer.

The sensations are too much for me. The smell of Holiday. The feel of Flint's blood on my shirt. The sight of myself stepping into the screen looming over us. Flint wrapping his hands around Holiday's neck and choking her. The taste of my own blood. I come inside her, again and again as I strike Flint with the telescope.

"You are not alone," Holiday breathes into my ear.

"I am not alone," I gasp when I'm finally done.

It's the first time in my life I've fucked anyone without a condom.

Holiday is gone the next time I wake up, but the video is still playing on its loop. I look in her wardrobe for some clean clothes to wear. All I can find are a pair of jeans and a Che T-shirt. I put them on and go out into the base to look for Holiday.

I'm not sure what time it is, but there are even more people on the street now. Some drink lattes from the woman's stand, others drink bottles of beer. I see Che sitting at a table with a lineup of people at it, entering their names into his laptop. I go over and ask what he's doing.

"Registering our new members," he says. He looks at my T-shirt and smiles. He finishes with the man on the other side of the table and waves the next man forward. "I think I need to hire an assistant," he says.

I look at the lineup. Some of the people are talking on phones, others are taking pictures of the base.

"Where are all these people coming from?" I ask.

"It's the videos," Che says. "They've gone viral. All thanks to you."

I don't know what to say. I listen to the people talk on their phones.

"You have to see this place," a woman says.

"Get everyone down here now," a man says.

"I haven't seen them yet, but the word is they're here," another man says.

I see a group of more men and women enter the base down at the end of the street. They stop and stare. I imagine they look like I must have looked the first time I came here.

All these people, just like me.

"We may need a bigger base," Che says.

I go to the latte stand for breakfast, but the woman is charging for her food and drinks now. I don't have any cash, and she doesn't accept credit or debit cards yet.

"I'm getting the wiring done next week," she says. "One of the new recruits installs lines for the banks. But I'm afraid it's cash only until then."

I head for work hungry. I keep thinking I should feel remorse after killing Flint. I should feel the way people do in the movies and be haunted by his ghost. But I don't. Every time I pass a store or coffee shop and see myself on a monitor, killing Flint, I feel better. I feel the hands of the people at the base on me. I feel the gaze of the people watching the monitor on me.

I feel more alive.

In the pod, I imagine myself—the real me.

Bedsheets float in the darkness above me.

I imagine myself in my bed. I hear someone singing downstairs. I get up and go down into the kitchen.

A glass pitcher floats in the darkness above me.

Holiday is in the kitchen, wearing one of my shirts. She's making breakfast. The table is set with three places. The pitcher sits in the middle of the table, full of orange juice.

A pair of running shoes floats in the darkness above me.

A boy in shorts and a T-shirt runs into the kitchen. He's

wearing the shoes. He hugs me, then Holiday. It's the boy from the HomeBrand commercials. That's when I realize I'm in the HomeBrand house. The boy sits down at the table and pours himself a glass of juice. Holiday smiles and hands me a plate of eggs and toast.

When Nickel pulls me from the pod, I don't feel hollow inside like I used to. I don't feel like anything in me is missing. I'm becoming the man of my dreams.

"Trotsky," Nickel tells me. "You're Trotsky."

"No, I'm not," I say and push myself back inside the pod.

Warhol. I'm Warhol.

After work I go down into the mall and buy new jeans and a new, blank T-shirt at a Gap. I throw the clothes I was wearing into the trash can outside the Gap. Then I go back to the base and Holiday.

I find her practising falls from the stage onto the floor below. She doesn't use a mat. Her arms are red from the impacts. She smiles when she sees me.

"I was hoping you'd come back," she says.

"Where else would I go?" I say.

We fuck in the bed again, as footage from her accident movies plays on the screen. When she comes, she rolls off me and catches her breath as she watches the videos. I finish myself off to the sight of her falling out of a taxi and rolling along the street.

We just lie there, holding ourselves, while the movies play. Holiday stands in the Mall Shooter theme range at Gun World. She's the Mall Shooter, taking aim at the cops hiding behind lottery kiosks and garbage cans on the video screens. But then she spins around as someone shoots her in the shoulder. The camera jerks a bit to follow her, and I have a glimpse of someone running away from the edge of the range. I think it's Che, but I'm not sure.

I look at Holiday's shoulder. There's a ragged scar there, like the path of a bullet grazing the skin.

"Is Che your boyfriend?" I ask her.

Holiday laughs. "Che doesn't know how to care about anyone but himself," she says.

"So there's nothing between you?" I ask.

She shrugs. "Nothing but Social," she says.

"What do you mean?" I ask, even though I know exactly what she means. But I don't want to believe it.

"He's a member there," she says. "That's how we met. Sometimes he requests me."

"Requests you for what?" I ask, but she shakes her head.

"I don't talk about my clients," she says. "It's unprofessional."

I let it go. I stroke the other scars on her body and she tells me how she got them.

A scar on her arm.

"I heated up the outside of an espresso maker in a Starbucks with a blowtorch," she says.

A scar on her leg.

"I glued a piece of glass to a revolving door in the mall," she says.

A scar on her head.

"I stepped into the path of a FedEx truck," she says.

"Why do you do accidents?" I ask. "Why don't you do something else?"

"Like what?" she asks.

"Real movies," I say.

"My movies are real movies," she says. "They're realer than real movies."

"You know what I mean," I say.

She's silent for a moment as she looks up at the screen. The accident clips have ended and it shows a blank video player now.

"I went to theatre school in university," she says. "I played Cleopatra. I played Hedda Gabler. I even played Hamlet. I was the star of every production we did. When I graduated, I got an agent. I auditioned for everything I could. I was going to be famous. Everybody else auditioning had been the stars of their productions, too. You know what roles I got?"

I don't say anything. I see where this is going.

"Shopper three in a grocery store commercial," she says. "Victim with a concussion in a workplace-safety training film. Pedestrian thirty-seven in a street shot of a film that was never even distributed. Extras."

I try to reassure her. "There's more to life than fame," I tell her.

"No there's not," she says. She sighs. "You know why I do the accident movies?"

"Because you're the star of those," I say.

"Because people *remember* me," she says.

I feel I should tell her something in return for what she's told me. I should share something secret about myself. I tell her about the vision I had of us in HomeBrand. I tell her about our son.

"You don't have to worry about that. I'm sterile," she says.

"Another accident," she says.

"You don't think I'd fuck you without a condom if I wasn't, do you?" she says.

I think maybe we could steal a child somewhere. Or maybe we could buy one, like that woman tried to buy me in the mall.

I go back to the condo where I killed Flint. I want to take what I can from the scene. I want to keep feeling the way I do. I want to make sure my illness doesn't return. Things that came into contact with Flint may help. The police will have cleaned up the scene, but maybe they missed something.

A bloodstained cushion.

An empty bullet casing.

The telescope stand.

I wear Flint's uniform. I think I'll probably have to break down the door, but no one's going to say anything to a cop at a crime scene. Only I don't have to break down the door. When I step out of the elevator on the condo's floor, I walk into a lineup of cops. They're waiting to get into the condo. The entrance is blocked by police tape and another officer, who lifts the tape to wave through the woman at the front of the line.

"Five minutes," he tells her. "Don't take anything, don't touch anything."

The others just glance at me. One of them waves me to the end of the line. I think about getting back in the elevator instead, but that may make them suspicious. I go to the rear of the line. I slip off Flint's name tag and put it in my pocket.

It takes only a few minutes to reach the door. The cops in front of me have already gone through the condo and left.

Other cops have come out of the elevator and joined the line behind me. I nod at the cop doorman, who studies me and then lifts the tape for me to pass. I go into the condo again.

The blinds are closed now, and Flint is gone. A halo of blood on the carpet where his head lay. A bloody line from the telescope beside it. A long strand of duct tape on the floor near where the camera had been. I want to pick up the duct tape and take it home with me, but I know I can't. Not with all these real cops here.

They stand around me, looking at the scene. Some of them close their eyes. One of them takes his gun out of his holster and then puts it back. All of them put their hands over their badges at some point or another. I put my hand over the bloodstains on my uniform.

I find myself standing beside the cop who took his gun out. He nods at me and asks if I'm going to the memorial.

"What memorial?" I ask.

"At Flint's place," he says. "It's going on all night. His wife is in charge."

"His wife," I say.

"Monaco," he says. He shakes his head. "She's destroyed by this."

Some of the cops kneel on the carpet before they leave and touch Flint's blood. I do the same thing. I know it's supposed to be cold and hard, but it's warm and wet to my touch. I feel Flint's heartbeat in it. I feel the heartbeat flicker and fade.

On my way out, I ask the cop at the door for directions to the memorial.

Flint's place is a condo in another condo tower only a few dozen blocks away. It's full of cops, too. It even has one at the door letting people in. I have a moment of déjà vu when he looks me over.

I go to the bar in the corner, where a man in a police dress uniform and white gloves is pouring drinks. He hands me a plastic glass.

"It's the same stuff from the scene," the man tells me.

"The same brand?" I ask.

"No, the same Scotch," the man says. "Drink up."

I sip the Scotch. It's the best I've ever tasted.

I look around the room, at the other cops, at the furniture, at the monitors on the walls playing slideshows of Flint.

Flint waving from behind the wheel of a cruiser.

Flint in a suit and tie, standing with a woman in a black dress. Holiday's dress.

Flint standing in the living room of this condo, smiling at me. Wearing the same uniform I'm wearing now.

Then I see her crossing the room toward me. The woman standing with Flint in the photo. His wife. Wearing another black dress, but this one much more formal. Holding a Scotch.

She stops and extends her hand.

"I'm Monaco," she says.

I almost tell her my name is Warhol, and then I remember where I am.

"Trotsky," I say, shaking her hand.

She looks at my clothes. At the bloodstains on them, the missing name tag.

"It's been a rough night," I say. I shake my head. "The paperwork."

"He always hated paperwork," she says.

"I know," I say, nodding.

I never really thought of her as real before. And here she is. I don't want to let go of her hand.

"Were you partnered with my husband?" she asks.

"He saved my life," I say.

Monaco takes a sip of her Scotch. "He seems to have saved the life of everyone here tonight," she says. "How did it happen?"

"A traffic stop," I say. "The man pulled a gun. But Flint shot him. If he hadn't, I wouldn't be here right now."

Monaco shakes her head. "He never told me about that. But he didn't talk much about work."

"He talked about you all the time," I say.

She looks down at her hand, which I'm still holding, and then back at me. "What did he say?" she asks.

I notice a few cops turning to listen. I think maybe I should be quiet. I shouldn't draw too much attention to myself. But I can't help it. I can see the pain beneath the surface of her face. I've seen it before in other people at accident scenes. People waiting to see if their loved ones are alive or dead. People just trying to hold themselves together. I want to see the pain come out.

THE WARHOL GANG 195

"Everything he did, he did because of you," I say.

And that's all it takes. Her face twists and then melts. She sobs and tries to break free of my grip, to cover her face with her hand. I pull her to me instead. I hold her in my arms.

"If you only knew what you meant to him," I say.

The other cops stand around me, silent, watching.

"It's all right," I say as she weeps into my chest. Into what's left of Flint. "I'm here. I'm here."

The next time I pass by the car in the mall, Thatcher is chasing the only other man who's still left. They move in slow motion, shuffling around the car, each of them keeping one hand on it at all times. The windshield is cracked now.

Thatcher goes back to the trunk and the other man moves to the hood. Thatcher follows him around the passenger side and the other man heads for the trunk. Thatcher reverses direction and the other man stops by the driver's-side door. Thatcher pauses by the front passenger door on the other side. They look at each other across the roof of the car, where the woman lies in the fetal position, shaking. They go back to circling each other.

I want to see what happens, but I'm late for work.

I go to the base again after work. I want to tell Holiday about the cops in the condo, about Monaco. But Holiday's not in the cinema. The screen is turned off. The lights on her makeup table are still on, though. I lie on her bed and wait. I fall asleep. She's still not there when I wake in the morning. I go out into the base but I don't see her in the crowd of people rushing off to work. I join them and head to Adsenses again.

Nickel holds a rampaging co-worker drill before we get in our pods. He calls everyone into the large meeting room. He wears a bulletproof vest like Flint's over his clothes and holds a plastic assault rifle. He hasn't shaved in days. He twitches sometimes while he talks. He tells us the rampaging co-worker drill is sponsored by the Sniper Bowl.

He lifts the assault rifle over his head. "This is the weapon of choice for the rampaging co-worker," he says, "but it's by no means the only one. Who had coffee from the staff room?"

Three people out of the crowd raise their hands. I don't put up my hand. I know better than to volunteer in a meeting.

"You're all dead," Nickel tells the people who raised their hands. "The rampaging co-worker poisoned the coffee." They put down their hands and look into their coffee mugs.

"The first thing you need to worry about," Nickel says, "is which one of your co-workers is likely to be the rampaging type." He tosses the gun up into the air. Everyone reaches for it but I'm the one who catches it.

"You have a minute to hide," Nickel says. "Then we'll begin."

People file out of the meeting room. One of the coffee victims puts up her hand. "Even us?" she asks. "Or are we still dead?"

"You're dead," Nickel says, "so you can just get to work."

"Do I still get to shoot them if they're dead?" I ask.

"That's entirely up to you," Nickel says. "If you think you'd be the type of person who enjoys mutilating the dead, then go right ahead."

I point the gun at the coffee victim and pull the trigger. It makes one of those fake machine-gun noises. "Now give me your purse," I tell her, but she just rolls her eyes at me.

"Not until the drill starts," Nickel says. "There's a procedure to these things."

We wait until everyone leaves the room, then Nickel looks at his watch. "All right," he says, "you can start shooting in ten seconds."

"Can I shoot you?" I ask.

"Why would you want to shoot me?" Nickel asks.

"Why wouldn't I want to shoot you?" I ask.

"Get out there and go to work," Nickel says, waving his hand at the door.

I go out into the main part of the office and look around. The cubicles are all empty. I wonder if everyone has left. Then the elevator door opens and a FedEx courier walks in, a package in his hands. He stops and looks at Nickel in his body armour,

THE WARHOL GANG 199

at me with the assault rifle. He tries to hide behind his package, but I shoot him anyway. The gun makes a rattling noise, and the FedEx courier screams, then looks down at himself.

I move on.

Behind me, Nickel tells the FedEx courier he should have run. "The people who don't run are the ones you see in body bags on the news," he says.

I go into the staff room and find Reagan. He's napping, his head down on the table. I put the rifle against his ear and pull the trigger. He falls out of his chair.

"I'm on break," he says, looking around from his place on the floor.

"You're dead," I tell him.

"Were you sleeping?" Nickel asks, coming into the room.

"You can't kill someone on break," Reagan says.

I continue on, looking for more victims. "The rampaging co-worker doesn't take breaks," Nickel tells Reagan.

I go through the rest of the office but can't find anyone else. I take the emergency stairwell up to the next floor. It used to be one of the abandoned offices. I'd played golf in there once with Nader and Reagan and Thatcher. We'd used light tubes from the fluorescents and balls of rubber bands. But now the entire floor is filled with pods like mine. I can't even count how many there are.

"You haven't looked in the supply room yet," Nickel says when he catches up to me. "Statistics indicate most people who survive office shootings do so by hiding in the supply room." He twitches some more and then hugs himself.

"How many of us are there?" I ask, looking at all the pods.

"You're not making effective use of your time," Nickel says. "In a real scenario, the police would likely be downstairs by now."

I go over to a window and look down at the street. I watch people go in and out of the mall with packages. I aim the rifle at a cluster of shoppers and pull the trigger.

"What are you doing?" Nickel says, looking out the window. "You can't kill those people."

"Why not?" I ask.

"They're not your co-workers," Nickel says.

"I'm rampaging," I point out.

"You should only shoot the people you know," Nickel says.

"Oh, I know them," I say, and pull the trigger again.

Holiday's still not at the base after work. It doesn't look like she's been in the cinema at all since I left. I leave it and run into Che coming out of the bank.

"I can't find Holiday," I tell him. "I'm starting to get worried."

"Don't worry about Holiday," he says. "She's waiting for us."

"Waiting for us where?" I ask.

"At our next mission," he says.

Our next mission is at a Holt Renfrew in the mall. Mao and Patty Hearst are waiting for us on the perfume floor, beside a display of naked mannequins intertwined in an orgy. I look around but don't see Holiday until she steps away from one of the counters, where she's been looking at various bottles. She's dyed her hair a deep red and she's wearing different makeup and a long coat, but underneath it she has on Flint's black dress again. I wouldn't recognize her but for that.

She stands at my side, and I don't know if I should kiss her or not. I want to, but she looks like a stranger.

"Where have you been?" I ask her. "I thought something had happened to you."

"I've been at Social," she said. "All sorts of things have happened to me."

"You don't have to do that anymore," I say. "I can give you money if you need it." I don't know how I'll come up with extra money, but I don't like the idea of her working there now that we're together.

"It's not about the money," she says. "It's about everyone requesting me since the Flint video. I've never been so popular."

"This is touching and all, but if we could get on with the mission?" Che says. He pulls a handful of Warhol masks out of his shoulder bag and hands one to each of us.

"What's this?" I ask, holding the mask and looking down at it. It's new and has none of the bloodstains of the one I wore before.

"It's our uniform from now on," Che says.

Patty Hearst and Mao both smile at the sight of the masks. Holiday just looks at hers without taking it from Che's hand.

"What uniform?" she says. "What are you talking about?"

"Rebranding," Che says. "The Warhol Gang has struck only twice and already it has better brand recognition than the resistance. So we're going to merge the two. We have to capitalize on the Warhol Gang."

"But there is no Warhol Gang," I point out.

"We're the Warhol Gang," Che says. He puts an arm around me and his other arm around Patty Hearst. He looks at each of us in turn. "We're all the Warhol Gang," he says.

Mao and Patty Hearst nod but Holiday still doesn't take the mask. "I wear the dress, not that," she says. "My character *is* the dress."

"You'll wear the mask if you want to be on the missions," Che says, pulling a camera out of his bag. Holiday looks at the camera but doesn't say anything else. She takes the mask and slips it into her purse.

"So what's the mission?" Patty Hearst asks.

"Chaos," Che says. "You guys wreck the place. I'll film it."

"What kind of mission is that?" I ask. "What about an accident? Who gets to be the victims?"

Che shakes his head. "That's not really the style of the Warhol Gang," he says. "We have to keep the brand consistency. It has to be an attack. Like with that cop."

"That was an accident, not an attack," I say.

"Accidents are what we do," Holiday says, pointing at the scars on her arms.

"We're done with accidents," Che says. "Accidents are for victims. And the Warhol Gang aren't victims."

"Shouldn't we put this to a vote?" I ask. "Aren't we a collective or something?" I look at the others, but they look at Che.

He points to the scar on his forehead. "When you've earned your place in the Warhol Gang like I have, then you can talk about voting," he says. "Now get started before someone notices us and blows the mission."

He's right: one of the women behind the perfume counters keeps looking our way in between helping shoppers.

"All right," I say. "What's the plan?"

"You're the plan," Che says, looking at me.

I stare at him, then at the others. They look back and forth between us.

"I don't understand," I say.

"We need a script," Holiday says.

Che doesn't turn away from me. He aims the camera at me.

"You're the one who keeps getting us on the news," he tells me. "Just dream up something like you always do." Then he leaves us, walking down a row of counters and disappearing into the crowd.

The others look at me again.

I don't know what to do, so I put on the mask.

And just like that I remember the video Paris showed me. The chemical accident at the warehouse. I think of the barrels of chemicals tumbling from the forklift and the men dropping to the ground, clutching at their throats, and then I'm grabbing bottles of perfume from the nearest counter and throwing them to the floor, shattering them. Breathing deep. Waiting for the burn, the moment I can no longer breathe. Waiting to fall.

The others watch me for a few seconds, and then Mao and Patty Hearst pull on their masks and start throwing bottles to the floor. Shoppers and clerks turn to stare. Within a few seconds, there's a pool of perfume at our feet.

"You are not alone!" Mao shouts.

"You are not alone!" Patty Hearst tries to shout but gags and coughs from all the perfume mingling in the air.

I have no idea why they're saying that. I look at Holiday. She shakes her head and throws her mask into the perfume pool.

The perfumes scorch my lungs. I breathe deeply and feel the rush of endorphins. I grab another bottle.

The clerk who'd looked at us before pulls a gun out from beneath her counter. She points it at me.

"Store security!" she yells. "Drop it!"

The edges of my vision fade away as I stare into the barrel of her gun, until all I can see is its darkness floating in front of me. My mouth turns so dry I can't speak. I wait for something to appear in the darkness but nothing does. I'm suddenly aware she's continuing to speak.

"—it drop it drop it drop it," she says.

I drop the perfume bottle to the floor. Everything turns white and then orange and black as the pool of perfume explodes. I stagger back as a fireball drifts up to the ceiling, igniting ad banners over the perfume counters as it goes. Screams all around me. My skin burns from the heat. Every breath I take is smoke. Then someone stumbles past me, on fire. It takes me a few seconds to recognize who it is. Patty Hearst. She lifts her blazing arms to me and I reach for her.

Che grabs me and pulls me away instead. He's holding me with one hand, holding the camera in the other. He's still filming.

Patty Hearst falls to her knees, then slumps into the burning pool. Fire all around us now. The sound of gunshots, or maybe bottles exploding. I can't tell, but flames spurt past us in all directions. Che stumbles back with me, past the mannequin orgy, which is burning now, too, the figures melting in the flames. I've lost sight of the others in the chaos.

Then the sprinklers open up and everything becomes a fog. I want to find Holiday, but I can't see her. And then even Che is knocked away from me by someone running past.

I duck underneath a table of burning credit card application forms and rip off my mask, stuff it into a pocket. When I stand back up, I can't see any of the others. All I can see are people I don't know, screaming and running for the exits, for the safety of the mall.

I join them and disappear into the crowd.

I find my way back to the base again. I discover it has more power now. Lights shine in all the store windows, and the broken glass has been replaced with fresh panes. The latte stand has moved to the gas station, and now there are other businesses, too. A woman sells clothes from racks in the dry cleaner's, and a hot dog stand has been set up at one end of the street, a crowd of people around it. A couple of men are renovating the inside of the general store. A sign in the window says Opening Soon. I wonder what it's going to be. People everywhere I don't know.

I sit on a pile of empty, broken-down Ikea boxes someone has discarded in the street and rest for a moment. I'm having trouble catching my breath. My throat is sore from the smoke, or maybe the perfume, or maybe both. My arms sting, and when I look at them I see some of the skin already starting to peel. My clothes are still wet and heavy from the sprinklers. I don't feel any of the usual things I feel after a mission. I just feel dizzy.

"Warhol," I tell myself. "You're Warhol."

But it doesn't help. I try to replay the mission in my mind, to find something to focus on to make myself feel better, but I just see Patty Hearst burning again.

I go into the bank and find Che sitting at a folding table covered in bottles of perfume. He's wearing a suit and tie now. A young man and woman dressed in office casual sort bottles at the other end of the table. They call out brands and put the perfume in shipping boxes. Che enters the information in his laptop.

The entire inside of the bank is nothing but folding tables piled with products. Cans of food. Stacks of sweaters. Boxes of phones. There's no furniture besides the tables and chairs. I thought Che lived here like everyone else in the base, but it's just an office or a warehouse or something. I wonder where Che's real home is.

"Who are all those people out there?" I ask Che, but he shakes his head.

"I have no idea," he says. "They just keep coming." He doesn't stop entering information into his laptop. "How did you know the perfumes would react like that and explode?" he asks. "Do you have some sort of chemistry training?"

"I saw it on a show once," I tell him. I look at the perfumes. "What's going on here?"

"While we were hitting the discount counters, another cell used the distraction to clean out the designer stock," he says. "We're rushing it to market while the demand is high." He shakes his head. "I can't even imagine what this is worth."

I pick up one of the bottles and look at it. There's ash on the glass. I wonder if any of it is from Patty Hearst.

"Keep it," Che says. "It's a collector's item."

"What do you mean, 'while the demand is high'?" I ask.

"The videos are already online," he says. "And not just mine. Someone posted the store's security footage. Now everyone wants a memento of the Warhol Gang's latest attack."

I look around the room again, then back at him. I feel like I'm collapsing into myself.

"What about Patty Hearst?" I ask.

Che looks at me. "What about her?" he says.

"What happened to her?" I ask. "Is she dead?"

Now the other two stop their inventory and look at me.

"We're in a war," Che says. "And you can't win a war without taking casualties." The others nod.

"What war?" I ask. "It was just a department store. You can't fight a war against a department store."

Che goes back to his inventory. "Take the perfume," he says.

"We should have taken her body," I say. But they're not listening to me now. They just keep on counting.

I pick up the bottle but it doesn't make me feel any better. I'm developing another immunity.

I go to the cinema. Holiday's sitting in the audience, watching *Panoptical*. She's watching us in the Holt Renfrew.

Mao throws a bottle of perfume to the floor.

Patty Hearts throws a bottle of perfume to the floor.

Holiday throws her mask to the floor.

The perfume clerk pulls out her gun.

I throw a bottle of perfume to the floor.

The screen flashes white with the explosion.

Patty Hearst runs flaming from the blast, and the camera turns to follow her. I want to reach out and touch her there on the screen, but then everything dissolves into a white mist as the sprinklers come on.

The video ends and Holiday hits a key on the laptop to replay it. I change into some dry clothes with Wal-Mart price tags still on them, then sit in a chair beside her. We watch the video again.

"It's not the same," Holiday says.

"Not the same as what?" I ask.

"Not the same as our other films," she says.

"Our other films didn't have crowd scenes with people on fire," I point out.

Holiday is silent for a moment, then says, "The camera followed Patty."

"She was the one on fire," I say.

"She shouldn't have been," Holiday says. "She was just an extra."

I reach out for her but she pushes my hand away.

"I didn't know that would happen," I say. "I don't know anything about chemistry."

"What is that supposed to mean?" she asks. She stares at me. "And what is wrong with your face?"

I climb back up on the stage and study myself in her mirror.

I have strips of what looks like rubber or plastic clinging to my face. I peel them off and inspect them for a moment before I realize what they are. Pieces of the Warhol mask have melted onto me.

I look back at Holiday in the audience, but I have trouble seeing her in the darkness.

"I'm supposed to be the star," she says.

I go to work and lie in the pod and imagine the scene from the Holt Renfrew over and over. I imagine grabbing a fire extinguisher and putting out the flames on Patty Hearst. I imagine holding her burned body. I imagine feeling the heat of her skin. The fluttering of her pulse.

I go into the staff room and find Nader buying things from the vending machine. He buys a bag of chips. He buys a granola bar. He buys a chocolate-chip cookie.

"I'm so sick of playing Thatcher," he says. "I'm so sick from playing Thatcher."

I wonder when it will be my turn to play Thatcher again. The thought of that makes me want to buy something myself.

"How about you?" Nader asks, tossing the chips and granola bar and cookie into the garbage can unopened. "How are you feeling?"

"I'm all better," I tell him.

"Because we have a special event coming up at Social," he says.

"I don't think I need that," I say.

"No one knows what it is, but the bartenders say it's going to be big," he says.

I try not to think of him with Holiday in one of the back-rooms, but I can't help it. I go to leave but the doorway I try to

walk through isn't really there. I hit the wall instead and acciden-
tally bite my tongue from the impact. I taste blood. I can't see
the real doorway. I feel the wall trying to find it.

Nader laughs as he watches me.

"Maybe you're not so better after all," he says.

The next time I go to the base, there are so many people there I can't tell it apart from the rest of the mall. I force my way through the crowd and into the cinema. Holiday's not there, but a surveillance video plays on the screen. A traffic camera. A car pulls up to a red light and stops. A man in a Warhol mask jumps into the frame, sliding over the hood of the car and opening the driver's door. At first I think it's me, that it's the video of the night I kidnapped Holiday, but then another man in a Warhol mask runs into the scene and opens the passenger-side door. The first Warhol pulls a man in a suit out of the car. The second Warhol pulls out a woman in a dress. The two Warhols climb into the car and drive away as the light turns green. The man and woman stand in the empty street, holding each other.

I go back out to the street and into a parade. A golf cart drives up the middle of the street. People step aside to get out of its way and then fall in behind it. Some of the crowd hold candles, others hold cellphones with pictures of candles on their screens. Che's driving the golf cart. A coffin is tied to the back of the cart with bungee cords. He honks the horn at me and slows as he drives past. That's when I realize it's not a parade. It's a funeral procession.

For a moment I can't breathe. I think it's Holiday in the coffin. I think something terrible has happened. And I wasn't there for it.

Che sees the expression on my face and shakes his head. "It's Patty Hearst," he says. "We're going to bury her."

"Bury her? Where?" I ask.

"In the graveyard," he says and keeps driving.

The base has a graveyard. I had no idea.

I join the crowd. A man I've never seen before nods at me. A woman I've never seen before puts her arm around me for a moment. And just like that, I feel like I belong again.

Che leads us to a dumpster against one of the walls. He gets out of the cart and pushes the dumpster aside to reveal double doors. He opens the doors. There's another chamber behind them. This one is small, maybe the size of a baseball field, with several support pillars for the mall rising up out of the ground, looming over the headstones scattered about. It's a real graveyard. There's dirt under our feet.

Che drives the golf cart to a dead tree in the middle of the chamber. The tree is decorated with Christmas lights. The extension cord disappears off into the darkness at the edge of the graveyard. Che undoes the bungee cords on the coffin and I help him lift it off the golf cart. It's lighter than I thought it would be. We put it down by the tree.

Then Che hops up on the coffin and turns to face the crowd.

"Patty Hearst sacrificed herself for what she believed in," he says. "Just like we've all made sacrifices." He points at the scar on his forehead. The people around me murmur and nod their agreement. I think back to the attack on the Holt Renfrew and wonder what Patty Hearst believed in.

"Patty Hearst sacrificed herself for the Warhol Gang," Che

says, looking at people in the crowd. "She sacrificed herself for you."

Again more people nod and say "Amen." I wonder if maybe there is a Warhol Gang after all.

Che climbs down off the coffin and puts his hands on it, closes his eyes. He bends down and kisses the coffin. Some of us cheer, others wipe tears from our eyes.

"You are not alone," someone in the crowd says, and then another person says it, and then everyone is saying it. Even me.

"You are not alone."

I wish I could open the coffin and see Patty Hearst inside. I wish I could have been the one to put her in there. I wish I could have been on the mission that stole the coffin.

We have a moment of silence, and then Che tells everyone to meet at the gas station for the wake. I ride back with Che in the golf cart.

"What was her body like?" I ask.

Che looks at me. "Whose?" he says.

"Patty Hearst's," I say.

"How should I know that?" he asks.

"Didn't you put her in the coffin?" I ask.

He shakes his head. "There's no one in that coffin," he says.

"You mean it's empty?" I ask.

"How would I get her body?" he says and shakes his head again.

I look back at the crowd following us. I wonder if they know the coffin is empty.

The gas station has been converted into a banquet area for

the wake. Tables are set up between the pumps, covered in plates of cookies, cakes, vegetable platters, bottles of beer and wine, Starbucks coffee jugs. There's even a table of the perfume bottles from the Holt Renfrew, with the date of the mission written on little cards attached to the bottles.

I'm trying to decide what to eat when Mao appears out of the crowd and grabs hold of my hands.

"Thank you," he says.

I look at him. I don't know what he means.

"That mission," he says, and then his voice breaks. He takes a moment to compose himself. "That was the most important thing I ever did with my life," he says. He squeezes my hands until they hurt. "It was the best thing that ever happened to me."

I don't know what to say to him. I'm still not even sure what happened in that Holt Renfrew.

Che puts his arms around both of us from behind.

"No," he says. "The best thing that happened to you is your new mission," he says.

Che takes us deeper into the underground of the mall on the funeral golf cart. We drive down access tunnels lit only by the cart's headlights. Rat skeletons and old shopping bags crackle under our wheels.

I wonder if we're anywhere near Social. I ask if we're going to pick up Holiday.

"Holiday's not part of this mission," Che says.

"But I've never done a mission without her," I point out. I don't know if I want to do this without Holiday. Whatever it is we're doing.

"Holiday can come on another mission when she believes in the Warhol Gang," Che says.

Mao looks back and forth between us but doesn't say anything.

I think maybe I should pass on this one. I'm not sure what's going on. But we're already on the mission. And I don't know where we are, anyway. I don't know how to find my way back.

Che stops at a doorway and turns off the cart's engine. We sit in the darkness.

"There are three trucks on the other side," he says. "Take the middle one."

"Take it where?" I ask.

"Get it outside," he says. "Find a parking lot somewhere. Then call me for the pickup."

"What should we do to ourselves?" I ask.

"What do you mean?" Che says.

"Should we drive the truck into a street light or a parked car or something?" I ask. "How do you want us to hurt ourselves?"

"You don't need to hurt yourself anymore," Che says. He tosses a new mask onto my lap. "Just find a parking lot."

We get out of the cart and he starts it up again, backs down the hallway.

"Remember," he says, "the middle truck. We need its cargo."

Mao and I watch the cart's lights fade away until we're alone in the darkness.

I know I don't need to hurt myself. I *want* to hurt myself. I want to feel everything I'm supposed to feel after I hurt myself. I want to feel alive again.

I think about walking away, about finding Holiday and doing more accidents with her, just her, and then Mao takes hold of my hand.

"You are not alone," he tells me. It sounds like he's weeping, but I can't tell because he's wearing his mask.

I put my own mask on and we go through the door and into a loading dock. The trucks are there, just like Che said. FedEx trucks. Mid-sized courier trucks, not the big transport trucks. I don't see any workers, but there are security cameras everywhere in the ceiling.

"We'd better hurry," I say.

We run over to the middle truck, but then we both try to get in the passenger seat.

"Aren't you driving?" I ask Mao.

"I don't know how to drive one of these," Mao says. "I thought you were driving."

"I don't know how to drive one of these either," I say.

We look at the truck for a moment and then hear voices from behind the door of one of the loading bays. We climb in the truck and crouch down out of sight, underneath the dash. I crawl behind the wheel. I see the truck is an automatic, so it doesn't matter which one of us drives.

The loading bay door opens. I lift my head to see who's there. I'm expecting security guards, but it's just a group of FedEx couriers drinking coffee.

"What do we do?" Mao asks.

I watch the couriers as they split up and hop off the dock. They head for the trucks.

"What do we do?" Mao asks again.

I look for the keys. There aren't any, but there's a green button on the dash. I push it as one of the couriers opens my door. The truck starts and he stumbles back, staring at me. At my mask.

He throws his hands up in the air and screams, dropping the coffee. I pull myself up into the seat. The other drivers stop getting into their own trucks and turn and stare.

I slam the truck into reverse and step on the gas. The truck accelerates backwards and I spin the steering wheel to turn around. The courier whose truck we're stealing runs to get out of the way. He doesn't stop screaming. Mao screams beside me. The rear of our truck smashes into the truck beside us, or the wall of the loading dock, I can't tell, but now there's the screaming of metal, too. I put the truck into drive and I spin the steering wheel the other way, step on the accelerator. We head for the exit.

We drive up a ramp to what I think will be outside, but it's a cargo road still inside the mall. Trucks travel in both directions. There are divider lines on the pavement and lights hanging from the ceiling overhead. A traffic light at our entrance. It's red but I turn on to the road anyway. Tires screech and horns sound behind us. I step on the gas pedal even harder.

"Where are we?" I ask, but Mao just shakes his head.

"Get us out of the mall," he says. "Che wants us out of the mall."

"I don't know how to get out of the mall," I say.

We're slowed down by a truck ahead of us. I wait for a break in the traffic coming the other way and then pass the truck. I can't see anything but more trucks and road ahead of us, and an intersecting road every now and then.

"Is there a map?" I ask Mao. He checks the glove compartment but shakes his head again.

I look around the truck. For the first time I notice a screen in the dashboard. It's blank, but when I hit one of the buttons underneath it turns on. A GPS.

"Destination?" a woman's voice asks.

I see flashing red lights reflecting off the walls behind us. I can't see the cops yet, but they're coming.

"Get us out of here," I say.

"Destination?" the woman's voice asks again.

"The nearest parking lot," I say.

"Turn right in fifty metres," she says.

THE WARHOL GANG 221

I remember Paris showing me the video of the truck smashing into the building, the bodies in the air.

I slam on the brakes as I see the intersection ahead. The connecting road is smaller, just one lane, and the truck bounces off the wall as I make the turn. It reminds me of the car chase with Holiday.

"We're losing the load," Mao says. I look in my mirror and see boxes tumble out the back of the truck.

"Che says we need those," Mao says.

"No time now," I say. "We're almost out." I nod at the light ahead of us. The end of the road.

"Turn left now," the woman says.

I look around, but there's no other road. There are just the walls of the mall around us.

"I can't," I say.

"You have driven past your turn," the woman says. "Please take the next left turn to get back on course."

"There are no left turns," I say.

The lights from a police car flash behind us again.

"Where are we going?" Mao asks.

Then I understand. We're still underneath the mall. The GPS can't read our depth. It thinks we're on the surface. Outside the mall.

We hit the end of the road and drive into an underground chamber. It's so large, I can't see the other side. The walls just fade away into the distance. It's some sort of garbage pit. Like the room I stumbled into after the security guards interrogated me, but much bigger. The road ends above the pit, but we're driving too fast to stop. I hit the brakes but I can tell we won't make it. I scream along with Mao as we go over the edge.

I have a glimpse of the garbage before the truck slams down into it. Bicycles, rotting produce, bent artificial Christmas trees, a jumble of naked mannequins. Then the windshield stars and disappears as we hit and I'm thrown forward.

The steering wheel stops me, knocking the breath out of me, but I see Mao tumble over the hood and into the garbage. He flails in it for a moment, but the truck keeps going forward, tilting over, falling upside down. On top of Mao. I think I hear him cry out again as the truck settles on him, but it could just be the sound of the cargo spilling out.

I've fallen up onto the roof of the truck's cabin now. I try to open the door but it's jammed. Garbage starts to spill in through the space where the windshield was. I climb out the driver's-side window before I'm trapped. And I start to sink.

The garbage sucks me down. Things shift underneath me, and I drop. Slowly, like quicksand from the movies. I'm being pulled deeper into a mass of torn yoga mats and discoloured couch cushions. I grab on to the edge of the truck, but then I see it's sinking, too. I look around for Mao but can't see him anywhere. I let go of the truck and reach out for a half-deflated beach ball instead. It starts to submerge into a sludge of rotten fruit.

Then I see a hand reaching down for me. I grab on to it and it holds me but doesn't pull me up. It's cold. I look higher up, at the face. It's one of the mannequins. They're not sinking. They're wrapped in each other's limbs like some sort of puzzle.

I pull myself up the arm, out of the garbage. Screeching tires on the ledge above me. I climb into the jumble of mannequins and cling to one of them, a naked woman. I listen to the voices above.

"We're going to need the barge," someone says.

"And the divers," someone else says.

Then I see it through a gap beneath me. A box from the truck, on the surface of the garbage. I reach down and pull it up. All that's left of Mao.

I look around and one of the other mannequins points the way out. A ledge with a door in the wall beside me. I crawl through the mannequins with my box. The mannequins shake and shift around me but don't sink.

"I think there's someone alive down there," one of the men above me says.

"That's just the gases," the other one says.

I open the door. Another dark tunnel on the other side. I pull myself into it and collapse on the floor. I try to open the box to see what's inside, but it's sealed too tight.

My phone rings so I pull it out of my pocket and answer. I think maybe it's Holiday. I want to tell her what just happened. But it's Mao.

"Help me," he says.

I look back into the garbage. I can't see him anywhere.

"Where are you?" I ask.

"I'm sinking," he says.

"Maybe you can walk out when you hit bottom," I say.

"I don't think there is a bottom," he says.

"Help me," he says.

I listen to him say it over and over until I lose the signal.

I pick up the box and look for a way out.

The tunnel ends in a stairway. The stairs go up and down, out of sight in either direction. For a moment I think about going down and searching for Mao wherever the stairs end. But I worry that maybe they don't end. Or I'll get trapped wherever he's trapped. So I go up instead.

I climb and I climb and I climb. I have to stop and catch my breath several times. When I finally reach a landing with a door, it doesn't open into the underground road, like I thought it would. It opens into the mall. I step out into a hallway with public restrooms. I take off my Warhol mask and leave it on the stairs. I go down the hallway and out into a food court. For a moment I think it's the same food court as the one with Thatcher and the car. It's identical—all the same outlets, the same layout, the same tables and chairs. Only there's no car, no Thatcher, no watching crowd. Just people ordering and eating their food.

I feel empty and drained after what just happened, so I buy a *venti* latte from a Starbucks and a *grande* Everything Burrito from a Burrito Planet. I sit at a table and put the box in the seat across from me. I look at it as I eat the burrito and drink the latte, but I still can't tell what's inside it. When I'm done my meal I try to figure out where I am.

I go back to the base. The wake is still going on, but it's turned into a party now. A DJ on the roof of the gas station. People dancing in the street. Some drinking, others taking pills. Some wear Warhol masks, some are naked. I don't recognize anyone from before. Maybe they're all new members. Or maybe there's something new wrong with my mind and I just can't remember them.

I go into the cinema, but Holiday still isn't there. Instead, there's a group of men watching a porn video on the big screen. A woman blowing three men. I can't see any of their faces. The woman looks out from the screen at me and moans as she switches from one cock to the next.

"Has anyone seen Holiday?" I ask the nearest man in the audience.

"Who?" he asks. He doesn't look away from the video.

One of the men on the screen gets on his knees behind the woman and starts fucking her. I see his face now. It's the man I was just talking to. But I still don't know the woman. I don't recognize the scene. I don't know what's going on here.

The woman on the screen looks at me and laughs.

I go into the bank and give Che the box. There are maybe a dozen people sorting through products on different tables now. The men all wear shirts and ties, the women business suits.

Che looks down at the box. "Where's the rest?" he asks.

"I think Mao's dead," I say. I tell him what happened.

He stares at me for a moment, then sighs and calls one of the men over.

"Schedule another funeral," he says. He looks down at the box. "And another mission. This won't be enough."

I wait until he opens the box. I want to see what's inside. I want something to remember Mao by.

But I don't want what's in the box.

Warhol masks.

Che pulls out a handful of them and holds them up to the light, inspecting them.

"You killed Mao for more masks?" I say.

"Do you know how many members are joining us each day?" Che asks me.

"We could have just bought more," I say. "I got my first one at a dollar store."

Che shakes his head. "They're gone as soon as they hit the shelves. You can't find them anywhere."

"But Mao is gone," I say.

"Don't worry," Che says. "We'll find another Mao."

I feel dizzy for a second, and I reach for the table to steady myself.

"What about Holiday?" I ask. "Can we find another Holiday, too?"

"Holiday is lost," Che says. He gives the box of masks to one of the women. "Holiday has always been lost."

I start to see the Warhol Gang in the pod.

A T-shirt with Warhol's face on it floats in the darkness above me.

I think maybe I'm hallucinating in the pod now.

Car rims with Warhol's face on them float in the darkness above me.

I close my eyes for a moment. When I open them again, a Warhol doll floats in the darkness above me. I scream until Nickel's voice asks me what's wrong.

"Let me out," I tell him. "I'm hallucinating."

"What do you see?" Nickel asks.

"Everything is Warhol," I say.

"That's what you're supposed to be seeing," Nickel says.

A sucker in the shape of Warhol's head floats in the darkness above me.

A porn video called The Warhol Gangbang floats in the darkness above me.

A Visa card with Warhol's face on it floats in the darkness above me.

"Consumer trends show it's going to be the next big thing," Nickel says.

I keep screaming, but Nickel doesn't let me out or stop the ads.

After work I go to Social to find Holiday. I look up at the camera over the door and imagine myself as Nader the time he was locked in his pod. The door opens and I go inside.

The place is packed, all the tables taken and people standing in every available space. I shoulder my way through the crowd to the bar and wave at the bartender.

"I want to see Holiday," I tell him when he comes over.

He shakes his head. "She's all booked up tonight," he says. "And there's a long waiting list."

I order a beer instead and drink it at the bar. When I'm done, I go into the back and look for Holiday.

I open the door to the basketball arena. A woman in a cheerleader's outfit dances for a couple of men sitting in the bleachers. It's not Holiday. They all look at me but the woman doesn't stop dancing.

I open the door to a clinic. A naked man is bound to an examining table with straps. A man wearing surgical scrubs takes the bound man's blood with a needle in his arm. They look at me but don't say anything.

I open the door to the office. Nader is there, lashed to a chair at a desk with neckties. Holiday stands behind him, strangling him with another necktie. She's wearing the black dress. They both look at me.

"What are you doing here?" Holiday asks me.

"I need to see you," I say.

Nader's eyes bulge. His face is red. He sticks out his tongue at me, although I'm not sure the action is voluntary.

"Everybody wants to see me," Holiday says. "You're going to have to wait your turn." She pulls the tie tighter around Nader's neck, and he makes noises I've never heard before, not even in the pod.

That's when my phone rings. It's Che calling.

"You are on a mission," Che says. "And it starts now."

"What kind of mission?" I ask, and Holiday looks at me.

"Put on your mask and get to work," Che says.

"But I don't have my mask with me," I say.

"No," Holiday says. "Not here." She twists the tie, bending Nader's head until he's staring at the ceiling.

"Pick somebody nearby and rob them," Che says. "Just be careful not to kill them."

"But the only person nearby is Holiday," I say. I decide not to mention Nader.

"Bring everything you take back to the base," Che says. That's when I understand he's not really talking to me. It's a pre-recorded message.

And then the screaming starts outside.

I leave the room and Holiday follows me. When she lets go of the tie, Nader gasps for breath.

"Please," he says. "I was almost there."

In the hall outside, I run into the cheerleader from the bas-ketball arena. She's wearing a Warhol mask now. She's carrying two wallets in one hand, a canister of pepper spray in the other. She aims the pepper spray at me but then stops when she sees Holiday.

"You are not alone," she says, although I can barely make out her words through the mask. Then she goes down the hall and into the main room of the club.

I look into the basketball room and see the two men writhing on the bleachers, rubbing at their faces. The sting of pepper spray in the air. They try to blindly high-five each other.

"I can't believe this," Holiday says over my shoulder.

We follow the cheerleader into the other room. The crowd has turned into a riot. People struggle with each other to get to the exit. Maybe two dozen men and women wearing Warhol masks point guns and designer Tasers and pepper spray and knives at people without Warhol masks. They take wallets and purses and pass cards from their victims. Everyone is screaming, except for the people who are laughing. Almost everyone is filming the scene with their phones.

"You are not alone!" a man wearing a Warhol mask shouts.

"You are not alone!" a woman wearing a Warhol mask shouts.

"You are not alone!" a man handing his wedding ring to a woman in a Warhol mask shouts.

"Not here!" Holiday shouts. "This is my audience!" She reaches into her purse and pulls out a gun. Flint's gun, from the night we killed him. She fires a shot at the ceiling. More screaming, and people push for the door even harder.

"What are you doing?" I ask.

"I'm taking my scene back," she says.

The Warhol woman taking the wedding ring from the man looks over at the sound of the shot. She opens fire with her own gun, just as Nader walks up to stand beside us, the ties still hanging from his neck and wrists. Blood hits the side of my face, and all three of us drop. I think maybe I'm hit, but I don't feel any pain. I look over at the others. Holiday lies face down on the floor. Nader stares up at the ceiling, blood spurting out of a tear in his throat.

More screaming and now people are fighting to get out the door, even the ones in Warhol masks. Someone yells "I'm not a victim!" over and over.

I climb over Nader to get to Holiday. He claws at me and I want to help him or at least hold him like I used to hold accident victims. I really do. But Holiday. I roll her over and there's blood on her face, her dress. I look for a wound but can't find one. "Where are you hit?" I ask.

She sits up and pushes me away. "I'm not," she says. "It's his."

We both look at Nader. He has both hands over his throat now but blood flows through his fingers and pools around his head. And now I do hold him.

When I look around the room again, I don't know how much later, it's empty. Even the bartenders are gone. It's just me and Holiday and Nader. She stares at the open door where everyone has gone. He stares up at the ceiling lights without blinking.

"We have to get out of here," I say. I know we have only a few minutes before the first emergency responders arrive.

"We have to find a new Social," Holiday says.

We hide out in the mall, in the You're History Experience, to avoid the security guards and cops. Holiday lies down in the Princess Diana crash scene, inside Princess Diana. Paparazzi circle us, taking photos of her body, as I try to rub Nader's dried blood off my hands.

My phone rings. Che. It's actually him this time, not a prerecorded message.

"What the hell was that?" he asks.

"Were you there?" I ask. "I didn't see you."

"I was watching," he says, then adds, "Do you have any idea what you've done?"

"It was your gang member who did it," I say. "She was the one who killed Nader."

"Who's Nader?" Che asks.

"She could have killed me," I say.

"I don't know who that woman was," Che says. "Maybe she's a member of Social. But she wasn't part of the team I assembled for the mission. We weren't supposed to kill anyone. Our contract said to just make them think we were going to kill them."

"What contract?" I ask.

"Our contract with Social," Che says.

"Social *paid* you for the attack?" I say, and Holiday sits up in the hologram. The paparazzi take more photos.

"We're going to have to give them a refund," Che says. "This wasn't the event they purchased. We can only hope they don't sue."

"What about Nader?" I say. "Are you going to give Nader a refund?"

"*Who* is Nader?" Che asks again.

"And what about Holiday?" I ask. "She could have been killed, too."

"Tell her she's fired," Che says. "And I'm putting you on temporary leave. You need to pull yourself together."

"Leave from what?" I say. "I don't want to be in the gang anymore." But he's already disconnected.

I put the phone away and tell Holiday what's happened. I ask her what we do now.

She lies back down inside Diana.

"Now we wait for the film," she says. "Now we find out who's the real star."

But there is no film.

We go back to my place and watch *Panoptical*.

Paris shows us a shootout between designers at a fashion show somewhere. The models wear Warhol masks.

Paris shows us a fight between two groups of youths on a schoolyard somewhere. They're all wearing Warhol masks.

Paris shows us a man in a Warhol mask robbing a gas station. On his way out he shoots the gas pumps.

Paris doesn't show us any films from Social.

"It'll take some time to get uploaded," I say.

"It should be up already," Holiday says. "It's breaking news."

We go to bed and hold each other. She won't take off her dress.

I dream we're lying in a bed in HomeBrand, only we're the couple from the ads.

When I wake up in the morning, she's gone from my arms. I go out into the living room and find her curled up on the couch with my laptop, still wearing the dress. She's checking *Panoptical* again. There's still nothing from Social.

"You can stay here for as long as you want," I tell her.

She looks at me and then back at the laptop.

I feel I should say something to welcome her into my home.

"I think I love you," I say.

"I know," she says without looking at me again.

I leave for work.

At the contest in the mall, it's just Thatcher and the woman now. The crowd is so large I have to stand on a table in the food court to see the car. Thatcher stands on the roof of the car, looking around. The woman hides under the car, hanging on to the bottom of it with her hands. The car is covered in dents now, all along the side panels and hood. The roof is buckled under Thatcher's feet. It looks like a total write-off.

Thatcher tries to say something to the crowd, but all that comes out of his voice box is static. The crowd cheers and takes more photos anyway. I take a photo of him with my phone. Then I continue on my way so I'm not late.

Nickel throws a going-away party for Nader. He holds it in one of the retro diners in the mall. The walls are covered with old street signs and photos. The booths are made from the frames of old cars.

All anyone knows about Nader's death is that he was killed in a bar shooting. No one says anything about Social. No one says anything about the Warhol Gang. I don't tell anyone what I know.

I sit in a rusting BMW with Reagan and a temp Nickel's made play the part of Thatcher. The temp's wearing a name tag that says Thatcher. He smiles at us and speaks in a buzzing voice, like he's trying to emulate Thatcher.

"We'd like to have the real Thatcher here," Nickel tells us, "but we can't stop the contest. There are so many people watching it now that they're selling space to advertisers."

"I'll be as real as I can," the fake Thatcher buzzes.

I don't want to be in this booth with Reagan and the fake Thatcher—I don't want to be at this party at all—but Nickel says it's important we keep the team together. He says we have to think of each other like family. I think now that Nader is gone I may have to play Nader. I order a beer.

Reagan looks at a hubcap hanging on the wall beside us. "I think I saw this in the pod," he says.

"What's a pod?" the fake Thatcher asks.

Nickel gives us a going-away card to sign.

"Who's this for?" I ask.

"Nader," Nickel says. "Try to keep your comments to ten words or less," he adds.

I open the card. It's full of the usual comments.

Wish you were here.

Enjoy your retirement.

Get well soon.

I write my comment in the card and pass it to Thatcher.

Sorry I couldn't save you.

"I think I saw this whole booth in the pod," Reagan says.

I hear cheering and look around. I see Nader standing beside Nickel in the centre of the room, waving at everyone. Only it's not Nader. It's a man who looks a little like him, who's even wearing the same clothes as Nader. But it's not him. I try to picture the real Nader in my mind as Nickel begins a speech about how the company won't be the same without him.

"Who is that?" I ask Reagan.

"I think it's an actor," Reagan says. "Or maybe Nader's replacement."

I stare at the fake Nader. "Do you think they have replacements for all of us?" I ask.

"I wish," the temp says.

Nickel finishes the speech and everyone applauds again. He hands Nader a gift-wrapped box. "From your work family," he says.

Nader has tears in his eyes. "I'm going to miss all of you," he says.

After the ceremony, Nader joins us at our booth. We all look at him and he looks at us. "You guys look like you've seen a ghost," he says and laughs.

"Are those Nader's clothes?" I ask.

"That's right," he says. "Because I'm Nader."

"Where did you get them?" I ask.

"From my closet," he says.

"Take them off," I tell him.

"What's the matter with you?" Reagan asks me.

"Look, I'm just trying to play a role here," Nader says.

Nickel comes over. "What's the problem?" he says, looking at me.

I shake my head. "I am not going to be Nader," I say.

I go home and there's blood on the kitchen floor. Not a lot—just spatters. But a trail of it. I follow it from the kitchen into the living room and then into the bathroom.

Holiday's taking a bubble bath. The bubbles are splashed with more blood. She's cutting at her arms with a paring knife from the kitchen, and for a moment I think she's trying to kill herself.

I grab her arm and try to take the knife from her, but she pushes me away.

"Don't worry, I'm not a real victim," she says. "This is what I do to relax."

I see now that the cuts she's making are shallow. There are a lot of them, but they're all flesh wounds. She's opening her old scars.

"How is that relaxing?" I ask.

"I don't know," she says, looking up at me. "But it makes me feel better."

I grab her arm again and try to make her drop the knife. She throws herself out of the tub and tackles me. We crash to the floor together. I hit my head on the edge of the sink and for a moment I can't move. Holiday cuts my shirt off with her knife. She runs the knife down my chest and we both look at the bloody line it leaves. I know without touching my head that there's more blood where I hit it. I push myself up, trying to throw her off, and she keeps me pinned there, slashing me some more with the knife, stripping the rest of the clothes off me. I finally manage to get the knife away from her when we kiss and I slide into her. We take turns cutting each other as we fuck on the bathroom floor. She stops me when I touch the knife to her cheek.

"Not the face," she says. "Never the face."

It's only when we're done that I notice the photos she's taped to the mirror.

Natalie Wood.

James Dean.

Marilyn Monroe.

Evelyn McHale.

We order out for pizza and salad and wine. While we wait for the delivery, I tell Holiday about my day, about Nader's going-away party.

"I know what happened," she says, looking out the window, at the mall's spotlights probing the clouds. "Che killed it." It takes me a moment to understand she's talking about the film of the Social attack. The film we haven't seen yet.

"He doesn't want to give me any more exposure," she says. "I was a star at Social. He's worried people may follow me again instead of the gang. So he's trying to disappear me. He's not going to post any movies. He probably bought everyone's camera and phones. I wouldn't be surprised if he deleted every copy."

"Why would he care if you're popular or not?" I ask.

She watches the spotlights in silence for a moment. Then she says, "Sometimes at Social he would pay me just to listen to him talk about his life."

"Like a therapist?" I ask.

"Kind of," she says. "Only he'd have me wear uniforms."

I think about Holiday in a cop's uniform. I wonder how much she charges for that.

"The problem with Che is he's never had a cause," she goes on. "He grew up middle class. There was nothing wrong with his life. He didn't need anything. But he needed *something*. So he found the resistance. And he stayed long enough to become the leader because it's all he has. But nothing he's ever done has mattered."

"What about his scar?" I ask. "The mission where he got that must have mattered."

Holiday laughs. "He got that at Social," she says. "An accident with a filing cabinet." She shakes her head. "Nobody cared about the resistance until it became the Warhol Gang. Now he finally has a cause. And Che's not going to let anything take that away from him. Including me."

"But what cause?" I ask. "I don't even know what the Warhol Gang is fighting for."

"It's fighting for itself," she says. "The Warhol Gang is its own cause."

"It doesn't matter now," I say. "We've got each other." I go to hold her hand, but just then there's a knock on the door. The pizza delivery. I get up to pay for it.

"I won't be deleted," Holiday says behind me.

I take Holiday on dates to try to distract her.

I take her to the apartment of a man stabbed to death in a robbery at the food court where the car contest is taking place.

We make ourselves dinner in his kitchen. We watch *Panoptical* on his laptop. We fuck in his bed. I wear his clothes to work. I come home and think Holiday isn't there, until she steps out of a closet behind me and puts the knife to my throat.

I try to imagine what the dead man did when he was stabbed.

"What do you want?" I ask her.

"I want it all," she says and cuts me some more.

I take Holiday to the apartment of a man drowned at the artificial beach in the mall.

We make ourselves dinner in his kitchen. We watch *Panoptical* on his laptop. We fuck in his bed. I take a bath and Holiday comes in and pushes my head under the water, holds me there until I pass out. I come to lying on the bathroom floor, her lips on mine.

I take Holiday to the apartment of a man buried alive when a dump truck loses its load of hot asphalt on him.

We make ourselves dinner in his kitchen. We watch *Panoptical* on his laptop. We fuck in his bed. We fall asleep but I wake to find Holiday trying to smother me with his pillows.

But it's not enough for Holiday. She keeps cutting and burning herself. And it's not enough for me either. None of these people's lives seem as real to me now as when I broke into places before. I want more than living in their homes. I want more than imagining myself as them.

I see more Warhol products in the pod.

A Warhol-branded gun with Warhol faces on the grips floats in the darkness above me.

I imagine myself back at Gun World, in the Urban Warfare theme range. I'm crouched behind a car on the street. I look at myself in the window and see I'm wearing a Warhol mask. I stand up and look around and a man at the end of the street shoots me. It's just like when Flint shot me—someone drives a spike into my chest and I fall to the ground and can't breathe. The world flashes red. I realize I'm one of the targets in the range.

A Warhol-branded BMW with a Warhol face in the BMW logo floats in the darkness above me.

I imagine myself standing in the doorway of the furniture store, waiting for Holiday. Our first mission. The light turns red and she drives up and stops beside me. I jump across the hood and pull open the door. She's wearing a Warhol mask. She takes Flint's gun from my hand and shoots me with it.

A Warhol-branded phone with a Warhol face on its back-plate floats in the darkness above me.

I imagine myself taking the photo of Thatcher at the car again. Only now Thatcher is wearing a Warhol mask.

That night I call up the photo of Thatcher on my phone, to remind myself of what he looks like. I'm lying in bed with

Holiday, after she choked me out with a plastic bag and I've come to again. She takes the phone away from me and looks at the photo.

"Where is this?" she asks.

"It's in the mall," I say and tell her about the contest.

"How many people are in the audience?" she asks me.

"I don't know," I say. "It's more every day."

She runs her hand over the screen, then turns and smiles at me.

"I know how we can make the Warhol Gang go away," she says.

"We'll steal the car in the mall," she says. "Just the two of us."

"Think of the exposure from all those cameras," she says.

"How will that get rid of the Warhol Gang?" I ask.

"It'll be the return of my character to a starring role," she says.

"People will want to know about the *Holiday* gang," she says.

"Everyone will forget about the Warhol Gang," she says.

I'm not sure about her plan, but we have to do something.

"Where will we take the car?" I ask.

"We'll work it out later," she says. "We'll work everything out later."

I think about HomeBrand.

"I think I know a place," I say. "We can start our own base."

"Whatever makes you happy," she says and slips the bag over my head again.

We go to the car contest in the mall. Thatcher is sleeping on the hood of the car, the woman on the trunk. Thatcher's clothes and skin are so stained in blood he looks as if he's been dipped in it. The tables in the food court are all sponsored now. We sit at the Test This! table. Stickers on the table advertise kits to fool urine tests for drugs. There are four flavours: Mountain Spring, Asparagus, Hung Over and Godly. I wonder what Godly tastes like.

Holiday wears her black dress. I wear Flint's uniform. His bulletproof vest, his gun. In my pocket is a Flint mask. It looks just like him, right down to the bloody wound on his head from where I hit him with the telescope. I ordered it online. It cost as much as my last paycheque. Holiday just shrugged when I showed it to her.

"As long as it's not Warhol," she says.

I wonder if I should change my code name to Flint.

Holiday's script says we're supposed to wait until people notice Holiday sitting there. Until they recognize her from her movies. Then I'll put on the mask and we'll take out our guns and hijack the car.

Holiday's script says everyone will film us then.

Holiday's script says we'll be the stars again then.

I don't care about being a star. I just want to make the Warhol Gang disappear. I want to make Holiday happy and start over somewhere. Just the two of us. And maybe some imaginary children. I think even if we can't have the real thing we can pretend to have the real thing.

But Holiday's script changes when the Warhol Gang attacks.

There are six of them. They come out of the crowd before anyone recognizes Holiday. They wear masks and dress shirts and ties and blank name tags. They point guns at the security guards, who lie down without being told. They duck under the caution tape and rush the car.

People around me scream and take photos as the gang grab the woman and pull her off the car, throwing her to the ground. Now it's only Thatcher. But then one of the gang grabs him and pulls him off the car, shoving him to the ground as well. He lets out a howl that crackles like feedback through his voice box.

Holiday holds her head. "I don't believe this," she says.

"What should we do?" I ask. I put my hand on my gun, but I'm not sure if I should draw it or not. I don't know what I would do with it if I did draw it.

"Nothing," Holiday says, dropping her hands and shaking her head.

The woman staggers to her feet. She's bleeding from a cut to her head and she wipes blood from her eyes. "Did I win?" she asks. She looks at the car and doesn't see Thatcher there and begins to scream in delight.

"Nothing?" I ask.

"If we get involved now, everyone will think we're still just part of the gang," Holiday says. "Extras."

"But we have to do something," I say.

Holiday shrugs. "What would Flint do?" she asks.

One of the members of the Warhol Gang breaks the driver's-side window with a hammer and unlocks the doors. They all get in. The driver ducks under the steering wheel for a moment, as Thatcher gets to his feet and charges back up the ramp to the car. The driver starts the car and puts it into gear as he sits up. The car hits Thatcher and knocks him down, rolls over him before the driver can stop it. I join in the screaming all around me.

The driver finally manages to hit the brakes, and the members of the Warhol Gang all look behind them, at Thatcher's broken body on the ramp. I run over to the car.

"What the hell are you guys doing?" I ask. "Did Che order you to do this?"

The driver looks at me. His eyes are wide behind the mask. "Who the fuck is Che?" he asks. Then the others yell at him that I'm a cop and they drive off, into the mall. The crowd parts to make way for them, people holding their phones to the windows to take more photos, like paparazzi.

I go to Thatcher. He lies twitching on the ground. He looks broken all over, and blood oozes from the corners of his eyes. Static comes from his voice box. I take his hand.

Holiday comes and stands beside me. She looks down at Thatcher, then watches the camera crews chase after the car into the mall.

"You are not here," I tell Thatcher. "You are not here."

After the paramedics take Thatcher's body away, we go back to my apartment and Holiday strips out of the dress and sits naked on the couch. She watches *Panoptical* and opens her scars. I don't know what to do. I think I have to stop this somehow. I go to the base to talk to Che.

The buildings have all been renovated now. The general store is an actual general store again, with signs in the windows advertising its products. Cans of soup. Fresh pasta. Cutlery and dishes. The dry cleaner's is an actual dry cleaner's again. There's a lineup of people waiting to pick up their clothes. Another building sells clothing—the front window is lined with Che T-shirts. There's even a Starbucks inside an old coffee shop. I see the woman who used to sell the lattes behind the counter.

I go to the bank to look for Che. It's a full-scale warehouse now, all shelves and boxes and even a forklift. Teams of people loading pallets and taking inventory. Che sits behind a folding table off to the side, smiling at something on his laptop. His assistant talks on her headset beside him, watching people work at a row of more tables. It's an assembly line. All the tables are covered with boxes and FedEx packages. A man takes a Warhol mask from a box and hands it to the man beside him, who slips it into a FedEx package with a piece of paper. He hands it to the next man, who puts it in a mail bag. There are maybe a dozen of them doing this, and several mail bags.

I pick up one of the pieces of paper. It's a contract. When I read it, I think I must be imagining all this. It says the purchaser of the mask agrees to the terms and conditions set out by the licensee, Warhol Industries. Trademark.

I take the paper to Che. His assistant puts up her hand to stop me but he waves her off.

"I always have time for Warhol after all he's done for us," he says, standing and walking around the table. He opens his arms as if for an embrace. "So you've come back to your family," he says.

"What is this?" I ask him, holding up the paper. I keep my distance.

"We bought the rights to the mask," he says. "You can't use one now without signing one of our contracts."

I don't know what to say. I stare at him.

"There were too many knock-offs," Che goes on. "We have total brand control now."

"Why did you kill Thatcher?" I ask.

Che drops his arms. "Who's Thatcher?" he asks.

I tell him about the attack on the car, but he shakes his head. "I don't know what you're talking about," he says. "That wasn't us. That's exactly why we need the contracts."

"What you need is to stop using the masks," I tell him, but he just smiles at me.

"You don't understand," he says. "The masks are only the

beginning. We're going to license every product we can. We already have a prototype catalogue. Coffee mugs. Tattoos. Ramen noodles."

"You're turning the resistance into Wal-Mart," I say.

The others look at me until Che's assistant clears her throat, and then they return to their work.

"Walk with me," Che says.

We go down the street, away from the bank. Che talks like he's giving a speech now.

"If we make consumers want what we have, we change the marketplace," he says. "If we change the marketplace, we change society. That's the true resistance."

We stop in front of a set of double doors in the wall, and I realize they're the ones that lead to the graveyard. My heart stutters a little.

Che looks at me, then back at the street and all its people. "The only question is whether or not you want to be a part of the new society," he says. "Whether or not you want to be a part of something greater than yourself. All you have to do is sign the contract."

I look at the paper in my hand. I don't want to be part of something greater than myself. I just want to be myself.

"We can still be your family," Che says, and his voice is softer now. "The only family you've ever truly known."

I don't know what to say, so I just walk away.

"Remember," Che calls after me, "you're not the only Warhol."

Holiday doesn't do anything but watch *Panoptical* and cut herself. She doesn't leave the apartment, she doesn't bathe. I'm not even sure she eats.

Paris shows us a group of men wearing Warhol masks rob a jewellery store. They smash the display cases with bicycle locks, and when they're done, they line up the store clerks and shoot them so they fall back into the displays.

Paris shows us a group of men wearing Warhol masks light all the vehicles in a car lot on fire. They shoot the video themselves. It looks like the BMW lot Holiday and I drove through before we crashed into the mall.

Paris shows us a man wearing a Warhol mask get out of a car that's been pulled over by a cop and shoot the officer as he approaches the car.

"They're getting more violent," Holiday says, tapping the knife against her leg. "That guy you worked with—"

"Thatcher," I say.

"Right. Thatcher was an accident. These are on purpose."

"The Warhol Gang has turned into a virus," Paris says. "And there doesn't seem to be any vaccine."

Holiday digs the knife in.

I have to do something. I listen to the scanner while Holiday watches *Panoptical*. I go out to a call about a man trapped in a recycling machine at a warehouse.

When I arrive at the scene, I find firefighters pulling the victim out of a baler, the kind that presses cardboard down into stacks. Bones stick through the man's skin here and there. He doesn't move on his own. I smell blood and breathe deep, but it doesn't trigger any of the feelings it used to.

The firefighters lay the body down on a stretcher, and I kneel between them. I take the victim's hand, but it's cold. When the firefighters notice me, I tell them it's all right, that I work here.

I don't feel anything at all in the man's hand.

The firefighters carry the victim away and I look around for something else, something I can take. There's nothing but a cop interviewing two men in overalls. When the cop steps aside to talk into his shoulder mike, I go over to them and ask what happened.

"We didn't see it," one of the men says. "We just heard him yelling."

"He hasn't been himself since his wife left," the other man says. "He kept talking about how he wished he was someone else."

"Well, I sure didn't recognize whoever it was they pulled out of that machine," the first man says, shaking his head.

The cop comes back and looks at me.

"Do you work here?" he says.

The other two men look at me, too.

"I thought he was with you," the first man tells the cop.

I go over to the baler and climb inside. I ignore the yells behind me and lie down on the cardboard. It's wet from the other man's blood. I can see more blood smeared on the press above me. I try to imagine the man's last moments. I try to imagine his life, but the cop reaches in and drags me out before I can.

I go home and find Holiday in bed asleep. When I sit down with my laptop, I find a video of a weatherman paused in the browser. We hardly ever go outside, so I don't know why Holiday would be watching the weather. I hit play.

The weatherman stands on a sidewalk somewhere and talks about growing pressure and the odds of lightning strikes. A man in a Warhol mask steps into the frame and points a gun at the weatherman. The weatherman tries to keep talking. He says something about breaking out the flowered shirts. But he stops when the other man puts the gun to his temple.

"Somebody help me," the weatherman says to the camera as the other man goes through his pockets with his free hand, taking the weatherman's wallet and phone. He takes the weatherman's wedding ring. He takes the weatherman's pass card. Then he tells the weatherman to take off his clothes.

"Please," the weatherman says. "People are watching."

"The forecast is not looking good for you," the man in the Warhol mask says.

"For those of you just tuning in," the news anchor's voice says as the weatherman starts to undress, "we're bringing you live footage of a robbery in progress. *Exclusive* live footage."

I don't want to get back in the pod and see more Warhol products. I call in sick the next day, but I can't stand being at home either. I leave Holiday there and break in to the apartment where I watched Miriam. The lock is still the same but all the furniture is different now. Leather couches and chairs, a futon instead of a bed, a bike in the hallway. The clothes in the closet are a man's.

I brush my teeth with the other man's toothbrush. I hide behind the couch and wait for him to come home. I listen to him unlock the door and walk inside. I listen to him piss in the bathroom and then change clothes in the bedroom. I listen to him get a beer from the fridge and sit on the couch. He turns on his laptop and watches *Panoptical*.

I get to my hands and knees and look over the back of the couch at him. It's the mailman who broke in to the apartment before. He's dressed in jeans and a T-shirt now, and he's not stealing anything, but I recognize him just the same.

I lie back down and wait. When he turns off his computer and goes to bed, I wait some more. When I hear him snoring, I get up and let myself out.

Back in my own apartment, lying in my bed and holding Holiday in my arms, I wonder if I dreamed up Miriam.

And then I'm mugged by the Warhol Gang.

I'm on my way home when it happens. A man and a woman wearing Warhol masks step out of an empty store and grab me, pull me inside. The man has a gun that looks just like Flint's service gun. He's wearing the same clothes I wore the night I killed Flint. The exact same clothes. The woman wears Holiday's dress. A fallen mannequin in the window wears a T-shirt that says Final Days—Everything Must Go.

"Holiday?" I ask, looking at the woman, but when I look at the man I don't know what to say.

She shakes her head as the man puts his gun to my temple and walks me behind some shelves.

"My name is Warhol," she says, pulling the sliding door shut.

I look into the mall for help, at the lingerie store across from us, but none of the women in it notice. They keep sorting through the discount bins.

"My name is Warhol, too," the man says. I don't recognize either of their voices.

The man kicks my feet out from underneath me and I fall to the floor, onto some empty garbage bags. He straddles me and puts the gun in my mouth, banging my teeth. The pain doesn't feel as good as it used to. I wonder what's wrong with me. It must be the masks.

"Get undressed," the man tells me.

I unbutton my shirt and take it off.

"Everything," he says.

I take off all my clothes. When I'm done, the woman gathers them up and puts them in one of the bags.

"Remember," the man says, "you are not alone." He takes the gun from my mouth and hits me across the face with it. I fall back and look at the dead fluorescents overhead.

I don't know if this was a message from Che or a random attack by some other gang.

I try to feel something, try to feel the rush of adrenalin and endorphins and everything that usually comes after I could have died. Instead, I find myself wondering if the man and woman signed Che's Warhol contract.

I roll on to my side and throw up on the empty floor.

I put on the mannequin's shirt and some painter's pants I find in a washroom in the back of the store. I use the shirt to wipe the blood off my face from where the man hit me with the gun. I go out into the mall again. I go home.

Holiday isn't cutting herself for a change. Instead, she's in the bathroom, putting on makeup. She's wearing the black dress again. I tell her about the mugging.

"Don't worry," she says without looking at me. "We're going to do something better than that."

"What do you mean, 'better'?" I ask. I take off the painter's pants and mannequin's shirt. I go to my closet and stand there, naked. I don't know what to wear.

"I've been researching video stats," she says. "The more violent the Warhol Gang films get, the more popular they are. We just need to make a more dramatic film and people will forget about the Warhol Gang."

"What do you mean, 'more dramatic'?" I ask.

I imagine a multi-car pileup.

I imagine everyone inside a Sony store lying dead on the floor.

I imagine Holiday and me falling from the window of a burning skyscraper, holding each other.

"We'll be the new resistance," Holiday says. She takes Flint's gun out of her purse and strikes a pose with it, studies her reflection in the mirror.

"How are we going to do that?" I ask.

She aims the gun at me. She blows me a kiss.

"We're going to take over the news," she says.

Holiday has found the address of the *Panoptical* studio. We drive there in my car. I wear Flint's uniform again. Holiday thinks it may help us get in the building. I have the Flint mask in my pocket in case I need a disguise. All Holiday will tell me about the mission is we're going to meet Paris. I think maybe the plan is to offer Paris an interview and tell her there is no Warhol Gang. Then I remember there is a Warhol Gang now. I don't know what we're going to tell Paris.

The studio is in an office tower in a row of office towers that are all clones of each other. We park in a lot across the street and wait. Holiday holds the gun Flint gave me for the carjacking in her lap. I have Flint's service gun in my holster. Holiday gives me a new camera from her purse.

"Whatever you do," she says, "keep the focus on me."

When Paris walks out the doors of the building, my heart pounds so fast I worry I'm going to have a heart attack. I can't believe it's really her.

"Action," Holiday says.

We get out of the car and cross the street. I put on the Flint mask. I turn on the camera and zoom in on Paris. I try to keep the image steady but my hands are shaking too much.

Paris glances at us when we step into her path but she doesn't stop. "You have to order autographs from the website," she says.

I feel dizzy being this close to her. A montage of all her disasters runs through my mind.

Holiday points her gun at Paris's face, and now Paris stops.

"Do you know who I am?" Paris asks.

"Do you know who I am?" Holiday asks, and Paris sees her dress now. She looks closer at me and sees I'm wearing a mask.

"I'm a big fan," I tell her as I film them.

Paris looks back and forth between us. "The Warhol Gang," she says.

Holiday shakes her head. "No," she says.

"Whatever you want, you can have it," Paris says. She offers her purse and I take it with my free hand. It's warm from her body. I want to open and go through it.

"But what we want is you," Holiday says.

"This is the script," Holiday explains to Paris, as we force her into the lobby of the *Panoptical* building. "You're going to get us into the studio. We're going to take everyone hostage. We'll lock them up somewhere."

"The supply closet," I suggest and they both look at me.

"Sure, whatever," Holiday says. She turns back to Paris.

"Everyone but you," she says.

"You're going to take us live," she says.

"We're going to execute you in front of the cameras," she says.

Paris stares at Holiday. I stare at Holiday.

"But why would you want to kill me?" Paris asks.

"We're not going to kill you for real," Holiday tells her. "I loaded my gun with blanks for the execution. But the bullets in his gun are real, so don't get any ideas."

We get into the elevator and Holiday tells Paris to take us to the studio. I expect it to be on the top floor, but she hits the button for the basement.

"Why would you *pretend* to kill me?" Paris asks.

"Ratings," Holiday says.

Paris studies her. "Ratings," she says.

"You make the news," Holiday says. "You *are* the news. Killing you gives us the attention we need to make sure everyone hears our statement."

"What statement?" Paris asks.

"There is no Warhol Gang," Holiday says.

"But if the bullets are blanks, she won't really be dead," I point out. "It won't be real."

"It doesn't matter," Holiday says. "By the time the truth comes out, I'll already be famous. People will remember the movie, not what actually happened."

Paris nods in agreement. "Killing me *will* get publicity," she says. "I'm the top-ranked site in the city."

Holiday smiles at her. "I'm glad you understand," she says.

"I do," Paris says. "But you don't."

We exit the elevator into an empty hallway. Paris takes us down the hallway to a blank door. She opens it with her pass card and we go inside. We're in a small room with green walls. A television camera stands on a pedestal in front of us. A spotlight hangs from the ceiling. They're the only things in the room.

I look around but there are no other doors. "Where's the studio?" I ask. "Where are the other people?"

"I don't know," Paris says.

Holiday puts her gun against Paris's head. "Don't make me execute you for real," she says.

"I just read the lines into the camera," Paris says. She looks at it like maybe it will save her. "They add everything else in at the main studio. It's CGI or something."

"Where?" Holiday asks.

"I don't know," Paris says again. "Somewhere in one of those Asian countries."

"This can't be happening," Holiday says.

"All the news shows do it," Paris says.

"What about the videos?" I ask. "The videos are real, aren't they?"

"Please," Paris says, "I'm just an actress."

Holiday doesn't say anything for a moment. Then she says, "How are you at improv?"

In the car, Paris sits in the passenger seat while Holiday drives. I sit in the back with the camera. I watch Paris through the view-finder. It's like she's in a show right in front of me.

"Don't worry about the studio," Holiday says.

"We'll take our show on the road," Holiday says.

"The whole world will be our studio," Holiday says.

I'm not sure which one of us she's talking to.

"You don't need me," Paris says.

"We can't do it without you," Holiday says.

We stop at a red light. Holiday rolls down her window and shoots at a man and woman crossing the street. They drop to the ground and crawl under a FedEx van on the other side of the intersection. Paris screams even though the bullets are blanks. The FedEx driver throws himself into the back of his van. When the light turns green, Holiday drops the gun back in her lap and drives on.

"Without you, that's just another anonymous drive-by," she says to Paris. "But with you, it's history."

Paris stares at her, then back at me, at the camera.

"Ask us questions," Holiday says as we drive.

"What kind of questions?" Paris asks.

"Interview questions," Holiday says.

"Look, I'm not even a journalist," Paris says. "I just read the lines they give me."

"You make stars," Holiday says.

"Like in your movies," I say.

"What movies?" Paris asks.

"All the videos you show us," I say.

"I . . ." Paris says and then doesn't say anything else.

"Those people were all just extras," Holiday says, "and look at what you made them. Look at what you made the Warhol Gang."

"And it doesn't even exist," I say.

Paris looks out the window, at the closed stores we pass.

"Imagine what you'll make us," Holiday says.

Paris opens the door and jumps out of the car. I swing the camera around to follow her as Holiday brakes to a stop, the car skidding across the median. Paris rolls a couple of times on the pavement and then gets to her feet. She runs in one direction, then stops and runs in another, like she doesn't know which way to go. And then Holiday screams, like she screamed when I drove into the mall our first time together. I turn back in time to see a taxi hit the front end of the car. I'm slammed forward, into the back of Holiday's head. I taste blood and then realize I'm lying on the car floor. The mask has been torn from my head and is gone. I reach for the camera but it's gone, too. When I sit up and look through the broken windows, I see it lying on the road.

I see the car is turned around backwards.

I see the taxi smashed into a parking meter on the sidewalk.

I see Paris lying on the street in front of a Payless Everything store.

I get out and stumble to her side. She doesn't blink or breathe. She's lying face up but her legs are twisted behind her. Her face is a shattered ruin: bloody and caved in, with a bone sticking through her cheek. A gum wrapper stuck in the oozing mess of her forehead. She looks like any other accident victim. Unrecognizable.

"Now what are we going to do?" Holiday asks, getting out of the car.

I put my hand to Paris's neck but I can't feel anything.

Holiday holds the back of her head and picks up the camera. Pieces of it are missing. She throws it down the street.

"Now what are we going to do?" she asks again.

I put my lips to what's left of Paris's lips and breathe. I taste her blood. I can't feel anything inside me. This isn't how I imagined kissing her.

"Call an ambulance," I tell Holiday, but she just shakes her head and leans against the car. She keeps shaking her head, like she's trying to clear her vision.

I reach for my own phone before I remember that the couple who mugged me stole it.

The taxi driver gets out of his car. He's holding a bundle of papers.

"I need to see your insurance," he says, walking over.

"Call an ambulance," I tell him. I can feel Paris's warmth fading. I'm already having trouble remembering what she looked like before the accident.

"I'm not calling anyone until we establish fault," the taxi driver says. "And I know the fault wasn't mine."

"You hit us," Holiday tells him.

"You crossed the line," the taxi driver says.

"Somebody call an ambulance," I say. I reach for my gun to force the taxi driver to get out his phone, but my gun isn't in the holster. It must have come out during the accident. I look at the window of the Payless, but I can't see anything there that will save Paris.

"You sign a statement saying it was your fault, and I'll call an ambulance," the taxi driver says.

Holiday reaches into the car and picks up her gun. She points it at the taxi driver but has trouble keeping it steady. "Do you have any idea who we are?" she asks.

The taxi driver looks at her but doesn't say anything.

Holiday looks around and then lowers the gun. "Get out of here," she says.

"What about the insurance?" the taxi driver asks.

"I don't know," Holiday says. "What are you worth?"

The taxi driver gets back in his car and drives off. The car squeals and leaves a trail of oil behind it. I imagine it won't be getting far.

"You shouldn't have done that," I say. I put my lips to Paris's again. "We need help."

"There's no one," Holiday says, gazing up and down the street. She takes a few steps one way, then a few in the opposite direction, like she's having trouble with her balance. "Not even a security camera."

I look at her. "What do you mean?"

"No one saw this," Holiday says.

I don't know what she's thinking. I pull Paris closer to me. But she's already gone. I can feel it.

"Help me get her in the car," Holiday says.

I drive while Holiday takes off Paris's jacket and goes through her pockets. The car shakes and makes little screeching noises every now and then, and there's dust in the air from the airbags, but it still runs. I didn't want to let go of Paris, but Holiday says she can't drive because she's seeing double since the accident. I wish I were the one going through Paris's pockets.

"We'll dump her body somewhere," Holiday says. "A parking lot. We'll get a new camera. We'll steal a new car. Hijack it. That will just add to the drama. Then we'll go back to the studio."

I'm careful not to drive too fast or run any lights. I don't want to be stopped. I can't imagine what the police would do to me for killing Paris. And I don't have anything to defend myself with now. I can't find Flint's gun anywhere in the car. It's gone.

"It's just a costume change," Holiday says.

I don't want to take Paris to a hospital. There's no point now. And the people at the hospital would ask too many questions. There would be security guards and cameras. But we can't just dump her anywhere.

"It's a big role, but I can pull it off," Holiday says.

I don't know what she's talking about. I don't care. I take Paris to the only place I can think of where it's safe to leave her. Adsenses.

Holiday finishes taking off Paris's skirt and looks up at the building. "What are we doing here?" she asks.

I tell her to wait in the car. I carry Paris in my arms into the elevator. She's almost naked now, wearing nothing but bra and panties. Her body is a mass of bruises. Another bone sticks out of her arm. Her legs flop in ways legs shouldn't move.

I bring Holiday's gun, too. Just in case.

I take Paris to my pod, but someone's in it. The door is closed and locked, and the man inside is screaming. I wonder who it is. I wonder if it's me. I wonder if maybe I'm dead. A ghost.

"I knew you couldn't stay away," a voice says from behind me. I turn and see Nickel.

Only it's not Nickel. It's Reagan, wearing the same clothes as Nickel. Wearing a name tag that says Nickel.

"I was expecting you to be alone," Reagan says, looking at Paris.

I lay Paris down on the floor and take the gun out of my holster. I point it at Reagan.

"I tried to quit once, too," Reagan says, ignoring the gun and glancing at my pod. "I didn't last much longer than you."

"I'm not coming back," I say.

"But here you are," Reagan says.

"I'm only doing it for her," I say, nodding at Paris.

Reagan looks at Paris again. "I don't think the pod will help her," he says. "I don't think anything will help her."

"I don't know where else to take her," I say.

Reagan studies me. "We can't save her, but we can save you," he says. "We can give you whatever you want."

I look around. It's just the two of us. The two of us and Paris. And whoever's in the pod.

"Where's Nickel?" I ask.

"I'm Nickel," Reagan says.

"You know what I mean," I say.

Reagan nods. "The position wasn't a good match for him," he says. "He's been transferred to Worst Case Scenarios."

"What's that?" I ask.

"It's one of our other divisions," Reagan says. "It's like us, only they see terrorist attacks and nuclear meltdowns and that kind of thing in their pods. He's much happier now."

It's only then that I realize Reagan has been smiling the whole time.

I shake my head and point at my pod. "Who's in there?" I ask.

Reagan doesn't answer. Instead, he turns and walks down the hall, into the room with all the monitors. I stand where I am for a minute, listening to the muffled screams, and then I follow.

Reagan sits by a pair of monitors showing scans of brains. He puts his hand on one of the screens.

"We've been showing him all the same ads you watched," he says. "We've sped up the process, of course. We cut down the time delay between them and eliminated all his breaks."

I watch colours flare and die on the screens.

"We've had some progress," Reagan says. "Some of the mapping is starting to parallel your scans." He nods at one of the brains. "But we have a long way to go yet." He cocks his head and listens to the sounds from the other room. "And not much time."

"Who's in my pod?" I ask again.

"Nader," he says.

"Nader's dead," I say.

"I mean the temp who played Nader," he says. "Although his name is Trotsky now."

"Turn it off," I say. "Let him out."

"He's our backup plan in case you didn't show," Reagan says. "But I knew you'd come back."

I look at the brains on the monitors again. I don't know what's going on.

"You'll never have to leave the pod if you don't want to," Reagan says. "We only ask one thing in return. You tell us what's coming next."

"What are you talking about?" I ask.

"Just tell us what the Warhol Gang is going to do," Reagan says. "Where it's going to strike. What it's going to steal."

I stare at him. I wonder how he knows.

"The analytics program saw it in your mind," Reagan tells me. "We went back and studied everything. We know what you've been thinking. We know what you've been doing."

"There is no Warhol Gang," I tell him, although I don't really believe that anymore.

"We can give you anything you can imagine," Reagan says again. "Drugs. Focus groups. Interns. We just want to be the first with the market research. We want to know what the War-hol Gang wants."

I point the gun at him again.

"You'd get a cut, of course," Reagan says. "We have a contract ready for you to look at."

"A contract," I say.

"Take it to your agent," he says.

"What's your motto?" I ask him.

Reagan pauses. "My motto?" he asks.

"What's your motto?" I ask him again.

"I'm in charge," he says. "What else would it be?"

I imagine firing the gun and a hole appearing in Reagan's cheek. I imagine blood and bits of brain matter spraying across the monitors. Then I realize I didn't imagine it at all. It really happened.

I lower the gun and look at the smoke coming from the barrel.

Holiday said the bullets in her gun were blanks.

The people Holiday shot at in the street, when we were driving with Paris.

The people we were going to shoot in the studio, if they'd been there.

Paris.

I walk to Reagan's side and look into his head. I can see bone and more blood and brain.

I leave Reagan in the chair and turn off all the monitors. I search through the desks in the control room until I find the name tags and a marker. I peel off Reagan's name tag and put a fresh one on his chest. Write a name. Trotsky.

I go back into the other room. I lift up Paris again. She's completely cold now. I wipe the blood from her lips. I want to put her in my pod, but I don't want to see the man inside it. I put her in Nader's pod instead. I hope she'll be safe there. I listen to the man scream some more and then I leave.

The video screens around the elevators are dark. For a moment I think they're turned off, but then I see little flickers of light here and there. Static. The screens are on, but they're not showing anything. They must be broken.

The doors open and I step inside.

I go back to the car and find Paris sitting in the passenger seat.

Only it's not Paris. It's Holiday made up to look like Paris.

Holiday has put on Paris's makeup.

Holiday has put on Paris's clothes.

Holiday has put on Paris.

I get behind the wheel and stare at her. "What are you doing?" I ask.

"We don't need her," Holiday says. "I can be her. I'll host *Panoptical.* I'll show everyone our movie from tonight. I'll close the episode with a twist: I'll take off her makeup and clothes. I'll become me again. Imagine the ratings."

I try to imagine none of this is happening. I try to imagine the bullets in the gun were really blanks after all.

Holiday takes the gun from me and slips it back into her purse.

A bus passes by. The ad on the side is for HomeBrand. It shows the family smiling in front of their house.

Your Last Chance to Live, the ad says.

The family is Holiday and me and the boy from the commercial.

I start the car.

"Take us back to the studio," Holiday says. "We can still do our show."

"We're going home," I say.

I head for the highway. I wonder how long it will be before someone finds Reagan's body and Paris in the pod and checks the security cameras. I've never seen security cameras in Adsenses, but I'm sure they're hidden somewhere.

I'll take us to HomeBrand. We'll break in to a house that hasn't been sold yet and figure out what to do next. Figure out how to pretend we belong. I explain the plan to Holiday as I drive.

"I'll go to a different placement agency and get a different job," I say. "I'll be a different person. You can play a different character. We'll be just like the neighbours."

"I have a different character now," Holiday says, gesturing at herself. "Take me back to the studio."

I try to ignore the ads I see on the billboards and bus stops we pass.

A black convertible.

A pair of sunglasses.

A camera.

Then I see the Ikea, and I turn into the parking lot.

"What are you doing?" Holiday asks.

I cruise the lanes, looking for a parking space.

"We need to buy things for our new home," I tell her. "Chairs. A bed. A dresser. Plates. Cutlery."

I try to remember if they sell clothes at Ikea. The ones I'm wearing still have bits of Reagan on them.

"If I let you get this out of your system, will you take me to the studio then?" Holiday asks. "Or do I have to carjack someone?"

I can't find an open parking spot so I just stop the car in front of the entrance. I get out and go through the doors. Holiday waits a moment, then follows me. She's walking a bit better now, although she still staggers every few steps.

I feel better as soon as I'm inside and surrounded by all the products. I want to sit in the display suites. I want to live the lives of the people they've been set up for. I want to stay in the Ikea.

But people turn to stare at us. At first I think maybe they're looking at the blood on my clothes. Then I see they're all watching Holiday.

"Paris," someone says. "It's Paris."

Holiday smiles and waves. "Remember, it could happen to you," she says. She grabs on to my arm to prevent herself from falling down.

We keep walking, past a row of fake bedrooms. People come out of the bedrooms to watch us, whispering to one another. Ahead of us, more people turn and stare. The crowd parts to make way for us.

"I should have been playing her all along," Holiday says.

I want to find things to buy, but I'm distracted by all the people following us. I wander into the kitchen accessories section and look at a set of knives. They're just like the one I saw in the pod, the same kind the woman used to kill her husband. The same kind Holiday used on me in Social.

"If they feel this way about Paris, imagine how they'll feel about me," Holiday says.

I want to ask her what she means by that, but then a young couple standing nearby ask if they can get a photo with her.

"Anything for my fans," Holiday says.

They stand close together in front of a wall of drinking glasses and the man takes a picture of them with his phone. I feel dizzy for some reason, and nauseous. I grab an Ikea shopping bag from a post and throw the knives in, then some forks and cutting boards. I take them straight from the display. I don't feel better just holding them, though. I hope I'll feel better when I pay for them.

"I can't believe this," the woman says to Holiday.

"It's all real," Holiday says.

"We'll be able to sell this for a fortune," the man says.

I look around and see other people taking photos. I see Ikea staff members watching us and talking on their phones. I look up at the ceiling and see security cameras.

"We need to go," I tell Holiday.

I think we'll drive to some other Ikea where people don't recognize her and get the things we need.

Another woman comes up to us and asks Holiday for a photo.

"I've seen every one of your shows," she says.

Holiday poses with the woman in front of a display of bowls and she takes a photo of them with her phone. "Which one is your favourite?" Holiday asks.

"The new one," the other woman says. "The one where the Warhol Gang kidnapped you."

"You mean the carjacking?" I ask, confused. "That's not new."

The woman looks at me. At my uniform.

"No, the one at the studio," she says. "The one from tonight."

"Where did you see that?" I ask.

"It's been playing everywhere," the woman says.

I grab Holiday. "We have to get out of here now," I say. I pull her deeper into the Ikea. Holiday keeps waving at the people we pass, and they keep taking photos.

We stop in the section with the beds and dressers. I see the cops ahead, hiding behind wardrobes and mirrors.

"They must have come in through the exit," I say. Holiday waves at the cops, too.

I turn to take us back the way we came, but there are more cops pushing through the crowd in that direction.

"We're trapped," I say. "There's no way out."

"I'll tell them you treated me well," Holiday says. "I'll put in a good word for you on the show."

I drop the Ikea bag and take the gun from Holiday's purse, hold it against her head.

"What are you doing?" she asks as the people around us scream. A man grabs my Ikea bag and dives behind a display of pillows.

"Improv," I say.

I back us away from the cops, who advance using dressers and bedside tables for cover. I drag Holiday over to the nearest Ikea clerk, who's trying to hide under a bed in a display. I crouch down and point the gun at him.

"Show us the way out of here," I say.

"There's only one way out," he says. "Just go to the cash registers."

"Find us another way," I say. "Take us to the staff room."

The clerk crawls out from underneath the bed and leads us to a door hidden behind a curtain display. I push him through the door and then Holiday.

"Don't follow us if you want her to live," I yell at the cops.

"Remember," Holiday says, "it could happen to you."

"Stop saying that," I tell her.

"But it's my motto," she says.

We're in an empty staff room. It looks the same as the staff room from Adsenses. A table, some vending machines, a garbage can. A monitor on the wall shows security-camera footage of the entrance to the Ikea. It's blocked off with more police cars than I've ever seen.

There's another doorway on the other side of the room. I ask where it goes and the clerk tells me the stockroom.

"Can we get out that way?" I ask.

"There's a loading bay, and some emergency exits," the clerk says. "But they all lead into the parking lot."

I look at the monitor again. "We need a disguise," I say.

"I don't," Holiday says, watching cops in body armour run into the Ikea.

"Take off your clothes," I tell the clerk.

"Look, there are probably some extra uniforms around here somewhere," the clerk says.

"I want yours," I say.

I put the gun on the table and tell Holiday to cover the clerk. I go to take off my uniform, but before I can, the scene on the monitor changes to inside the Ikea. I see now it isn't security-camera footage at all. It's a news show. A reporter talks mutely into the camera. Behind her, the cops build a barricade with the wardrobes and dressers. Past them is the door to the staff room.

"We're live," Holiday breathes.

I reach for the remote on the table and turn up the monitor's volume.

"—could happen to her, it could happen to anyone," the reporter says. "It could happen to you."

"No," Holiday says.

I turn back to the Ikea clerk, to make him show us the way out, but he's already gone. All that's left of him is his clothes. The door to the stockroom is open, and I see rows of shelves stretching away into a vanishing point.

"That's my line," Holiday says.

I look back at the monitor and see the door to the staff room open and Holiday walk out, into the showroom. I see the cops wave her to them. I see a cop step from behind a mirror and reach out for her. It's one of the cops from the car chase, the one with the bandage around his head in the Paris interview. He's still wearing the bandage.

"It's the hostage," the reporter says. "It's Paris."

I look away from the monitor and at Holiday. I can't see her in the lights from the cameras outside. I look up at the monitor again and see Holiday raise her gun and shoot the cop reaching for her. The cop falls back into the mirror, crashing to the floor with it.

"Paris has joined the Warhol Gang!" the reporter cries.

"No," I shout, but it's too late.

"My name is Holiday!" Holiday says. At least, I think that's what she says. Her words are lost in the gunfire from the other cops.

Blood sprays from Holiday's body and she spins around and hits the wall. She slides to the floor and lies in the doorway.

The cops stop shooting.

No one moves.

"Remember, you saw it here first," the reporter says. "Paris's death, live."

I grab the gun from the floor. I fire several shots around the edge of the door, then pull Holiday back into the staff room and slam the door shut. I flip the table onto its side and hide behind it as bullets come through the walls. I hold Holiday in my arms and her blood runs out over my hands. She convulses and looks up at me. She's been shot in the face. Her right cheek is nothing but a hole. I can see shattered teeth through it, the gore that's the back of her throat. Her eyes are wide. She grabs on to me. I wouldn't recognize her now if I didn't know her. She looks like just another victim.

"No," she says. "No no no no no." Then she chokes on the blood filling her mouth.

"You are not alone," I tell her. "You are not alone."

Her eyes stop moving. She keeps looking at me, but I know she's gone. I've seen this enough times.

"Please," I say anyway. "I'm not letting go."

The firing stops and I look up at the monitor. Cops edge

along the showroom wall toward the staff room. I try to shoot the monitor but the gun is out of ammo.

I lift Holiday in my arms and stagger into the stockroom. I don't want the cops to shoot me in the back so I turn at the first intersection of aisles, then the next. I hear yelling and gunfire somewhere behind me, but I don't stop.

I wander around for maybe ten minutes before I realize I have no idea where I am or where I'm going. The aisles don't seem to have an end. I look around at the shelves for some sign, but they just hold stacks of blank boxes.

I carry Holiday for as long as I can, and then I fall with her.

I lean against a shelf and cradle her in my arms. I stroke her hair. She doesn't move. She doesn't breathe. She doesn't even bleed.

I find an empty spot on one of the shelves and lift her into it.

"You are not alone," I whisper to her again.

I pull boxes in front of her, until she's no longer visible. Then I look for a way out.

I don't know how much longer I wander the aisles before the lights turn off and fire alarms ring. For a moment I can't see anything. Then I see a red glow floating in the darkness in the next aisle over.

I push aside some boxes and climb through the shelving. An emergency exit sign hangs from the ceiling overhead in the new aisle. I go in the direction it points. Another emergency exit sign at an intersection tells me where to turn next. I follow the signs through the stockroom, until I come to a door in the wall.

The door has one of those red handles that warn an alarm will sound if pushed, but I don't think I have anything to lose at this point. I open the door. It leads into the parking lot. The alarm joins the other alarms.

I think about going back for Holiday, but I don't even know how I'd find her now.

I close the door behind me, and the alarms fade.

I wander through the parking lot until I see more cops running into the Ikea. I think maybe I should join them. I should help search for Warhol and the other gang members. Then I remember I'm not Flint.

I go over to where a man is loading boxes into the back of a minivan. I point my gun at him but he just looks at me.

"I don't think I'm the one you're looking for," he says.

"You're exactly the one I'm looking for," I say. I grab him and push him toward my car, which is still parked in front of the Ikea, surrounded by police cruisers. "Get behind the wheel and wait for the cops to find you," I tell him. "Tell them your name is Warhol."

"But *you're* a cop," he says, looking at my uniform.

"I used to be a cop," I tell him, "but I'm not anymore."

He looks at me a moment longer, then heads for the entrance. Once he's in the next lane over, he runs, dodging between cars and ducking. He goes past my car and through the Ikea doors. I'd shoot at him if I had any bullets left in the gun. Instead, I just watch him disappear. Then I get in the driver's seat of the minivan. The keys are in the ignition. A woman sits in the passenger seat, talking into a phone. She looks at me, then at my uniform just like the man did. Then she looks into the back of the van.

"Hang on a minute," she says into the phone. "What's going on?" she asks me. "Where's my husband?"

I think about taking her with me. I close my eyes and try to imagine what's in the boxes in the back, but I can't see anything.

"I'm your husband," I say, but I can't imagine our life together.

I don't open my eyes again until I hear her get out and run away.

The police have set up a roadblock at the entrance to the Ikea to stop people from getting in. A long lineup of cars stretches back to the highway, waiting. The cops leaning against their cruisers just glance at me and the boxes in the back of the minivan.

"Evidence?" one of them asks, and I nod. They wave me through.

I try to imagine driving the minivan into them and pinning them against their cars.

I try to imagine getting out of the minivan and shooting them with their own guns.

I try to imagine walking down the lineup of cars, shooting the driver of each one.

But I can't imagine anything.

I think my mind is broken.

I drive off into the night.

I head out into the suburbs. I still want to find HomeBrand. It's all I can think about. I'll figure out what to do next while I hide out there with Holiday and our son.

I shake my head. I don't have a son. I don't have Holiday. I'm alone again.

And I don't know where HomeBrand is.

The van has one of those help buttons, like the truck Mao and I stole. I hesitate before using it, but I don't know what else to do. A woman's voice speaks to me through a hidden speaker after a few seconds.

"Hello, Mr. Benedict," she says. "How may I assist you?"

"What's my full name?" I ask her.

"You're Mr. Lester Benedict," she says. "A gold customer. Your wife is Mrs. Dora Benedict. Your children are River and Stone."

"What do I do?" I ask.

"You are a software engineer," she says. "You are a gold customer."

"Where do I live?" I ask.

"Are you in distress?" she asks. "We have preferred emergency response for gold customers."

I try to imagine my life as a software engineer. My wife and kids. My home. But I can't imagine any of that either.

"Show me the way to HomeBrand," I say.

She directs me into a maze of subdivisions, where the houses all look like each other. The children's bicycles and inflatable balls on the front lawns all look like each other. I'm lost within minutes.

But then we emerge from a row of dark houses onto an empty street. Now there's nothing but the foundations of houses on either side. Holes in the ground.

"You have arrived," she says.

"What is this?" I ask.

"This is HomeBrand," she says.

"The GPS must be off," I say. "There's nothing here."

"The GPS is accurate," she says. "You have arrived at Home-Brand."

I get out of the minivan and go over to the nearest hole. The ground around it, where a lawn or a rock garden or whatever should be, is hardened mud. Pieces of rebar and wood are stuck in it. Nails and screws. I look into the foundation for the house. It's full of water, with a layer of slime on top. Like a forgotten swimming pool.

I turn around and see the sign on the other side of the street. HomeBrand. Now Building.

It shows the couple from the ads, but someone has spray-painted Bankrupt! over their faces.

I look down the street. It stretches away in a straight line, toward a cluster of smokestacks far in the distance. Nothing but empty lots the whole way.

"Mr. Benedict?" It's so quiet I can hear her voice from the minivan. "Are you in distress?"

I get back in and close the door. I do a U-turn.

"Take me back to the mall," I say.

She leads me back across the highway and to the nearest mall entrance, a stairway that descends into the ground in the middle of a parking lot. There's no building, not even a sign. Just the tunnel going down. I park in front of it but don't get out.

"Is there anything else, Mr. Benedict?" the woman asks me.

"I don't know," I say. Then, after a minute, I ask, "What's your name?"

"You named me Dora," she says. "But you may edit my name if you like."

"What do you mean?" I ask.

"Dora was the name you chose for me in the registration process," she says. "But you are free to change that in the preferences menu."

"Are you real?" I ask her.

"Define real," she says.

I get out of the minivan. I leave the engine running, the door open. I leave Dora calling my name. Calling Benedict's name.

I go back down into the mall.

I try to go to my apartment, but cops with body armour and assault rifles stand in front of the mall elevators leading up to my building. Their rifles are just like the one Reagan used at Gun World. I stay at the rear of the crowd that's gathered.

Camera crews film the cops. People in the crowd take pictures of the camera crews. I think someone must have found Reagan and the security footage in Adsenses already.

"You are not alone," someone beside me says. When I turn to look, a man pulls a phone out of his pocket.

"You are not alone," the phone says. A ring tone.

The man runs up to get in front of the cameras. "Do you see me?" he asks.

One of the elevators opens and everyone turns to look. Some of the cops aim their assault rifles. But there's no one inside. The doors close again.

"Do you see me now?" the man on the phone asks.

I go deeper into the mall, down into the depths of the discount stores and pet shops, in search of a place to hide. Instead, I find a funeral procession going through the mall. I can tell it's a funeral procession because of the golf cart with the coffin strapped to it.

Behind the cart, the line of mourners stretches out of sight. There are people wearing Warhol masks, and other people with Warhol masks painted on their faces, like kids at carnivals. Women here and there wear black dresses like Holiday's. I see a number of men with shaved heads and barcode tattoos. People wave phones and cameras in the air, recording the action. A man in a Starbucks apron spray-paints Resist! on the window of every store he passes. The clerks come out to watch, but no one tries to stop him or any of the others.

I look at the driver of the golf cart and see it's Che's assistant, the woman with the headset. She's talking into the headset right now as she drives. She has a cut on her head. It's in the same spot as the scar on Che's head. I fall in beside her and look at the coffin. I wonder if it's a funeral for Holiday. I lay my hand on the coffin but don't feel anything other than it's plastic, not wood.

"Who's in there?" I ask Che's assistant.

She looks at me. "There's no one in the coffin," she says.

"I mean who's the funeral for?" I ask her.

"It's for Che," she says.

I look back at the coffin, then around at all the people. "What happened to Che?" I ask. I think I must have misheard her.

"He was martyred," she says.

"A new gang member shot him," a man in a shirt and tie says. "He said he wanted to be famous."

"No, it was an undercover cop," a man in hospital scrubs says. "They infiltrated us before the raid."

"Raid?" I ask.

Che's assistant nods. "They've seized the base," she says. "But it doesn't matter. We'll make the whole mall our base. That was Che's plan anyway."

"It was mall security," a woman in a FedEx uniform says. "They paid for the hit."

"So where is Che?" I ask the assistant.

She taps her headset. "He's in here," she says.

I stop and they keep walking past me, filling the hall, a never-ending army.

"You are not alone," they say over and over.

I go back to the base. I want to see if Che is really dead. I think maybe I imagined the funeral procession and I'll find him alive. I think maybe I imagined the last few days and I'll find Holiday waiting for me in the cinema.

But there are new people in the base, setting up tables in the street, setting up lights on the tops of buildings. Running large fans to clear smoke from the air. I cough from the lingering scent of pepper spray. At first I assume they're cleanup crews from the police or whoever was responsible for the raid. Then I see film cameras, and people with headsets and little lenses hanging from lanyards around their necks.

I go over to one of them, a woman who's directing two men to scratch the windows of the dry cleaner's with sandpaper. "It has to look real," she says.

"It is real," one of the men says.

"Realer than real," the woman says.

"What are you doing?" I ask.

The woman glances at me and then back at the windows. "The other cops are in the cinema," she says. "Tell them to hurry up. We need to get our props in there soon."

I go down the street and into the cinema. I want to see what they're doing in there.

The air is smoky inside, and there's no light but the flashlights of two cops. The seats are melted lumps, and there are scorch marks up the walls. The screen has been burnt away entirely, leaving only an empty hole on the charred stage now. The smoke makes me cough some more, and the cops shine their flashlights on me. They're plainclothes cops—one wears a Che T-shirt, the other a John Lennon T-shirt—but I can tell they're cops from the badges on chains around their necks.

"I'm here to help," I tell them. Reflex. They look at my uniform and nod.

"We're done with everything here, I think," Lennon says. "But you can come along to the penthouse with us if you want. There are truckloads of stuff still to inventory there."

"The penthouse?" I ask.

"Che's place," Che says.

I ride in the back of their car. It's unmarked and looks like any other car, but inside a transparent shield separates me from them. It's like watching a cop show. It's like being in a cop show.

We park in front of a condo tower that has a doorman. He opens the car door for me and I step out onto a carpet on the sidewalk. Che tosses the doorman the car keys.

I look up at the building. It's so tall I can't even see the top.

There's a private elevator that goes up to the penthouse. It's operated by a pass card Che takes out of his pocket. It has a photo of Che on it. The real Che, not this one.

The elevator doors open directly into the penthouse suite. I step into the room and it's like stepping into the pod come to life. The penthouse is the same as the one I imagined in my first vision in the pod, right down to the white furniture and mirrors on the wall. I stop and stare. I touch the wall to make sure it's real.

"What is this place?" I ask.

"This is the head office," Lennon says. He goes into the kitchen and takes a beer from the refrigerator. "Make yourself at home," he adds.

I glance around for the woman talking on the phone I imagined before, but I don't see her. I go over to the mirror and look at my reflection. I see myself but I don't feel anything. I don't feel that hollowness inside, I don't feel a flush of adrenalin. Nothing. I turn and look out over the city. I can't see my apartment building.

Che goes into a bedroom. It's full of boxes instead of furniture. I don't want to look in them in case they're full of Warhol masks, but he opens one and shows me its contents. Vibrators. He opens another box. Wedding bands in small plastic bags. He opens another one. Phones.

"The guy's place is a warehouse," Che says. "We thought at first he was some kind of professional thief, but then it turns out he was working for a company."

"A company?" I ask.

Che nods at a laptop sitting on a stack of boxes. "He has all the inventory and the memos in there," he says. "They gave him orders for hits on places. Some numbered company. A price for a name."

"$3.141," Lennon says from behind me.

"That's the one," Che says, opening more boxes and peering inside. He takes a bundle of credit cards from one and puts them in his pocket.

I stare at them. "What did you say?" I ask.

"Pi," Lennon says, taking a drink of his beer. "The number that doesn't end."

"Looks like the whole Warhol Gang was just some kind of corporate thing," Che says. "One company would pay him to attack another."

I open the laptop. The desktop image is a collection of

THE WARHOL GANG 301

Warhol masks of different skin tones. Black, Asian, Mediterranean. There are red-haired masks, and bald ones. The word "prototype" is stamped across each of their foreheads.

A row of folders occupies one side of the screen. I scan their names. Inventory. Staff. Vacation Requests. Orders. Completed Missions. I open the Completed Missions folder. It contains a list of memos. I open the one called Holt Renfrew.

From: Che

To: $3.141 Project Manager, Megastores

Subject: Mission Taking Stock a success. Invoice will follow.

It's dated the same day we attacked the Holt Renfrew.

I close the laptop without looking at any of the other memos. I want to throw it out the window. "I don't believe this," I say.

"If you don't believe that, you should see what he has in his bedroom," Che says. He goes down the hall with Lennon and they disappear into one of the other rooms, but I don't follow them. Instead, I go back to the elevator. I'm worried it won't work without the pass card, but the doors close when I hit the button for the main floor. My vision strobes. I try not to black out.

In the lobby, I ask the doorman to bring the car back. He parks it in front of the building and holds the door open for me. When I get in, he looks down at me.

"Do I know you from somewhere?" he asks.

"You don't know me," I say.

"Have you been here before?" he asks.

"I'm nobody," I tell him and close the door.

I go back to the placement agency. I sit in the waiting room and watch a live news report from inside the Ikea on the monitor on the wall. I watch the same reporter that was there before, when the cops killed Holiday.

Dead. Holiday is dead.

"Police say they have arrested several members of the Warhol Gang on the scene and continue to search for Paris," the reporter says. She's standing in the Ikea staff room now. Bloodstains on the floor and the open door to the stockroom behind her.

"Police say the gang members were working at the Ikea and had been planning this operation for months," the reporter goes on. "Apparently they intended to commit a mass murder-suicide when Paris showed up, but authorities were alerted by a customer inside the Ikea and arrived in time to stop their plans."

I wonder if any of that is true.

"Police say Paris may have been a member of the Warhol Gang all along," the reporter says. "She may have been using her show as a recruiting tool. Police haven't found her yet and aren't sure if she's alive or dead."

I glance at the other people in the waiting room but none of them look at me. They just keep watching the monitor.

The placement officer is a new person. A blind man. He wears headphones attached to his computer. He stares sightlessly at me and asks me what I want. He wears a name tag that says Vegas.

"What happened to the other one?" I ask.

"The other what?" he says.

"The other Vegas," I say.

"Is this a work issue?" he asks. "Or a personal issue?"

"I want a new job," I tell him. "I want a new life. A new identity. Can you get me plastic surgery?"

"That's not the sort of thing we do," he says.

"You're the ones who got me into this situation," I say. "But I don't know how to get out of it."

He asks for my ID number and looks me up in the system. His keyboard looks normal to me but he tilts his head and listens to the headphones rather than reading the screen.

He turns his head and stares at me with his sightless eyes.

"We can't help you," he says.

I pull out the gun but it doesn't matter. He can't see it. He just keeps talking.

"You're no longer one of our temps," he says.

"What do you mean?" I ask.

"You've been hired away from us," he says.

"Who hired me?" I ask.

"Adsenses," he says. "They've made you a full-time, permanent employee."

I put the gun away again. I try not to cry.

"Congratulations," the placement officer says.

When I go back to the waiting room, Flint is talking to the reporter on the monitor.

"We know there are more members of the Warhol Gang out there," Flint says. He turns to gaze into the camera. "They could look like you. They could look like me."

I go back into the mall.

I see Holiday walking toward me with a Gap bag. She looks in the windows of the stores she passes. I stop and stare at her, but she walks past without noticing me.

Only it's not Holiday.

I see that when I look closely at her. Her hair is the same colour and style as Holiday's was when we did our first mission, the carjacking, and she's dressed all in black. But it's a black suit, not a dress. And her face is different. I've never seen her before. I watch her disappear into the crowd.

Farther down the hall, I see another Holiday come out of a beauty salon. She has the same hairstyle, too. She's wearing a black dress, but it's a casual one, not Holiday's formal dress. She talks into Holiday's phone. But she's much thinner than Holiday, and younger.

I wonder if maybe I could imagine one of these women as Holiday, if I could live a life with one of them.

I go into the salon. Women sit in all the chairs in the back, getting their hair styled. A poster on the front of the counter advertises the Warhol Cut. It shows a picture of Holiday in a street somewhere, Flint's gun in her hand, gazing up into the camera.

The woman behind the counter asks if she can help me.

I grab the next woman who walks out of the back of the salon looking like Holiday. I pull out my empty gun and put it into her side. I drag her into the mall.

I take the new Holiday with me to the You're History Experience. I don't know where else to go now that I've seen there is no HomeBrand.

Holiday begs me to let her go as we walk.

"I have a husband," she says. "A child."

"No, you don't," I tell her. "Not yet."

I think I can hide with her in the holograms. We'll kiss, like before. We'll forget everything that happened in the past. But when we get to the You're History Experience there's a new hologram. The Ikea.

Cops crouch behind their furniture barricades, pointing their guns at the door to the staff room. Someone has spray-painted the word Resist! on the door. Shoppers hide farther back, holding up their phones to film the scene. I stand behind them and stare. The door opens and Paris walks out. She looks just like she does on *Panoptical*. There's no sign of Holiday at all now.

"No," I say, because I know what's about to happen. I want her to turn around and go back inside the staff room. But instead Paris just smiles as she looks at all the people watching her. The cops relax and smile back. A couple of them even wave.

"The Warhol Gang has let Paris go," the reporter says from behind her barricade.

Paris shoots the cop who steps from behind the mirror and

THE WARHOL GANG 307

reaches for her. "You are not alone," she says. He falls back into the mirror, crashing to the floor with it. Pieces land at my feet. I can't see myself in them.

The cops shoot Paris, and she spins around and hits the wall. She slides to the floor, leaving a smear of blood on the wall. I try to shoot the cops with my gun, but it's still empty. I hear the new Holiday scream beside me, but then it's lost in the screams of everyone else in the Ikea. I watch a man wearing a Warhol mask and Ikea uniform come out of the staff room and shoot at the cops, then drag Paris away. I scream myself.

The hologram fades and I'm alone in the room. Nothing but blank walls. The new Holiday is gone. If she was ever there in the first place.

I don't leave. There's nowhere left to go. When the hologram starts again, I step into it.

The display bins of the Ikea are lined with products I saw in the pod.

A toaster.

A blender.

A knife block.

When Paris steps out of the staff room, I try to grab her, to hold on to her, but my hands go through her. She shoots the cop who steps out from behind the mirror. Flint. The other cops open fire and she falls. The man in the Warhol mask drags her away. The scene fades and I'm left holding air.

When the hologram starts again, I try to look through the doorway into the staff room, to see myself in there. But it's only

empty space, a void. Then the man in the Warhol mask materializes where I'm standing and shoots at the cops. He drags Paris
away again and the cops return fire. The scene fades to nothing.

I try to change the scene. I close my eyes and try to imagine
someplace else. I try to imagine myself as someone else, someone not trapped in a hologram Ikea shootout. All I can imagine
is myself back at the first accident scene I went to, the one at
the abortion clinic.

I imagine holding the dying man trapped under the car.

I imagine the dying man as me. He looks up and tries to
speak, but no words come out of his mouth.

I don't know who I am.

I try to shut out the sounds of the real cops arriving in the
room.

"Warhol!" they shout. "Drop the gun, Warhol!"

"Trotsky," I say. "I'm Trotsky."

I open my eyes. I'm still in the Ikea.

"Warhol!" the cops keep on shouting.

The man in the Warhol mask materializes where I'm standing and shoots at the cops.

The cops return fire and everything fades away.

Acknowledgements

I would like to thank the Canada Council for its support during the writing of this book. I would also like to thank Anne McDermid and Vanessa Matthews of the McDermid Agency and Iris Tupholme of HarperCollins for believing in me. A very special thank you goes to Kate Cassaday and Jennifer Lambert for their patience during the editing process—and for asking the questions that really needed to be asked. Finally, I would like to express my gratitude to all those readers who contacted me with kind words about my writing and demands for a new book. I couldn't have finished *The Warhol Gang* without you.